GOING DOWN FAST

NEW YORK TIMES BESTSELLING AUTHOR

CARLY PHILLIPS

Copyright © Karen Drogin 2016
Print Edition
CP Publishing 2016
Cover Photo and Design: Sara Eirew

Billionaire Bad Boys: Rich, Powerful and sexy as hell.

Lucas Monroe dropped out of college only to become a multi-billionaire and tech world God. He can have any woman he desires in his bed, but the only woman he's ever wanted is off limits and always has been. When Maxie Sullivan finds herself in dire straights, the only man she can turn to is the one she's always secretly loved: her childhood best friend.

Can they trust their hearts and make a future, or will their complicated pasts stand in the way?

This bad boy is going down fast …

And going down fast has never felt so right.

**"Carly Phillips is synonymous with red-hot romance and passionate love."
—Lauren Blakely, NY Times Bestselling Author**

* * *

Prologue

L UCAS MONROE WAS at the top of his game. As the
co-creator of Blink, the social media app that had
taken over the world, and with a recently successful
IPO on Wall Street behind him, he was now getting
ready for a night with a gorgeous model any guy would
kill to date.

He put down the razor and dried his face with a
towel, finishing up with a pat of cologne, his gaze
drawn to the tattoos he'd had done that traveled down
one arm and marked his side. He'd gotten the ink after
he'd started working out and bulking up, determined
to be a different man than the insecure kid he'd once
been. He'd come a long way from the nerdy high
schooler who was afraid to ask a girl out—one girl in
particular—and who stammered over his own name.

Tonight he was headed to the Polo Bar, a popular
night spot his date had chosen and, thanks to his

connections, they were able to get in. Personally, he could live without the whole need-to-be-seen thing, but if it meant getting laid, he'd put in the time.

He dressed in a pair of black slacks and a white button-down shirt, rolling the sleeves. Just as he grabbed his keys and was about to leave, his cell rang.

A quick glance and his stomach twisted with a familiar pang. He answered immediately. "Hello?"

"Lucas!"

"Maxie, what's up?" he asked his beautiful downstairs neighbor.

"It's the baby," she said, her voice shaking and tearful. "I need you."

All thoughts fled except getting to her as soon as possible. He raced down the stairs, not waiting for the elevator, and rushed through the hall. Her door had been left open, he assumed for him, and he let himself inside.

"Maxie?" he called out.

"In here."

He strode toward the sound of her voice and found her standing in the hall bathroom, blood covering her bare legs beneath her maternity dress.

Panic and fear rushed through him at the sight, and he froze in place. "What happened?"

"I don't know," she said, tears in her eyes. "I was putting the baby's crib together."

Lucas narrowed his gaze and catalogued that piece of information to deal with later. Like why wasn't the baby's father doing that job?

"I got tired," she went on. "So I went to lie down and I woke up to… *this*." She gestured to the blood with shaking hands.

"Let's go." He stepped up to her, wrapping an arm around her and carefully leading her out of the small room. "I'm taking you to the hospital." He managed to sound strong and in charge when, in reality, the blood had him completely panicked.

She stopped in her tracks. "But I called my doctor. I'm waiting for him to get back to me and tell me what to do."

Lucas frowned at her calm tone. "Well, he can damn well find you in the ER. What do you need?"

She pointed to her purse on a chair in the family room. "I'll grab a towel from the bathroom," she said softly.

"I've got both." He went for the towel, then her bag, and returned quickly, herding her to the door.

A few minutes later, he'd hailed a cab, and they were in the backseat, Maxie huddled close. She clung to him, plastered to his side, her breathing heavy.

"Oh my God, what if I lose the baby?" she asked, her voice muffled in his shirt, which was now damp with her tears.

Pure fear had taken over her earlier calm, and he was almost relieved. Her lack of reaction before had been freaking him out. He'd had a hard enough time hiding his panic.

HE STROKED HER hair, feeling the hard press of her belly against his side. "It's going to be okay, baby. Hang on," he said as he silently prayed for her to be all right too.

Meanwhile, she cried soundlessly beside him, shaking. And breaking his heart.

"Can't you hurry up?" he asked the driver he'd already promised a hefty tip to get them there *fast* and safe.

"Doing the best I can in this Manhattan traffic, buddy," the older man said. But he cut off a car in the next lane and hit the accelerator harder.

Finally, the car screeched to a stop at the hospital emergency room entrance. Lucas threw a fifty at the driver and helped Maxie out of the cab.

One look at the blood on her legs and towel and the triage nurse grabbed a wheelchair. Lucas held her hand, rushing beside her.

"How far along are you?" the young nurse asked.

"Almost seven months," Maxie whispered. "It's too early."

Lucas squeezed her shoulder. They reached a set

of swinging doors and the nurse paused. "Are you her husband?" she asked.

"No but—"

"Wait here. I'll come out as soon as I know something."

"But—" Lucas cursed himself for not lying through his teeth to go in with her, but he hadn't been thinking about anything except Maxie. And the blood.

The notion of losing her for good was unbearable. He refused to think about the fact that he'd already lost her in the only other way that mattered.

"No, he can come with me," she said, sniffling.

"We don't know what the situation is. I promise once you're stabilized, I'll come get him," the nurse said, turning the chair so she could back herself and Maxie through the entrance.

He met Maxie's tearful gaze as she was wheeled away, the big doors closing behind her, leaving him to wait. Alone.

MAXIE WOKE WITH a start, and a cloud of depression immediately cloaked her in fog. She didn't have to think to know the world as she knew it had ended. She blinked and tears streamed down her cheeks unchecked.

"You're awake."

Lucas. She forced herself to roll to her other side and face the man who'd done everything he could to help her. Without success. The blood had been a shock. The debilitating pain had begun almost as soon as she'd entered the hospital. The rest was a horrific blur of words the doctor had used, each one an agony-filled stab in her heart. Late-term miscarriage. Nothing she could have done to prevent it and nothing she *had* done to cause it. Probably due to chromosomal abnormality. Rare occurrence. I'm sorry.

"Maxie? I asked if you're okay? I mean—"

"I know what you mean."

Lucas was worried about her.

"I don't understand. I wish…" Her voice caught on an unexpected sob.

Lucas was by her side in an instant, pushing his big body onto the small hospital bed along with her and pulling her close. He smelled delicious, a citrusy masculine scent. It comforted her. *He* comforted her and she burrowed in closer.

"The nursery's all painted, the crib nearly done. I named him—" She choked back a cry.

"Let it out," he said, holding on to her tightly.

He was so solid. So there. Unlike her husband, who, from the minute she'd seen blood, was nowhere to be found. He hadn't even returned her call. She hadn't checked her cell since being in here, but she had no doubt Lucas had tried to reach him.

But it wasn't Keith she needed now, it was Lucas, and true to form, he was there. The one to make her feel better when she was hurting, the one to comfort her when she had problems. He'd been her next-door neighbor since they were ten years old, her best friend, the one she could count on, always. But when her teenage feelings had changed, deepened, she'd kept them hidden.

Good girls didn't make a play for boys, her very religious mother had hammered into her. And Lucas, well, he'd been different back then. Less confident. He hadn't acted on any change in dynamic between them either. The timing had never been right. *They* had never been.

"Lucas…"

"I'm here, baby. For anything, I'm here."

"I know. And thank you."

The tears began again, the thought of the fear when she'd seen blood, the sheer panic when she'd realized she was alone. Her absolute refusal to face what was so obviously happening. She'd dialed Keith, but her heart had wanted Lucas, and when her husband wasn't reachable, she'd called the one man she knew she could count on.

"I don't know what I would have done without you." She'd dampened his shirt but he didn't seem to care.

He merely shifted, wrapping his muscular arms

7

around her tighter. "You're strong. Stronger than you know. You'll get through this," he reassured her. "And I'll be here for you. Whatever you want or need."

The distinct sound of someone clearing his throat sounded, and she jumped, her gaze darting toward the door to her room.

"Isn't this cozy?" Keith slurred, lounging in the doorway, glaring at Maxie and Lucas, who stiffened but didn't make a move away from her. "Your message said it was an emergency, but looks like situation normal to me." He made his way into the room, weaving slightly on his feet.

God, she didn't need this right now. Her husband was obviously drunk. His clothes were wrinkled, and there was a noticeable red lipstick stain on his collar.

Under any other circumstances, she'd want to die of embarrassment, that Lucas was seeing what her marriage and life were really like, but she'd lost the only thing that mattered and that had bound her to Keith. She couldn't bring herself to care about his feelings now.

"I'll handle him," Lucas whispered into her hair.

"No need to handle anything, *brother*," he sneered. "I'll handle my own wife."

Maxie closed her eyes and let the tears fall. For the baby she'd lost and the life she could have had… if only she hadn't married the wrong brother.

Chapter One

Nine months later

LUCAS POURED HIMSELF a cup of much-needed coffee after a ridiculously late night with Derek and Kade, his best friends and partners in Blink. He brought the drink to his mouth only to be interrupted by a knock.

He placed his cup on the counter and headed for the door, swinging it open, shocked to find his sister-in-law standing on the other side. As usual, he forced himself to use the term he'd had to get used to over the years—because it put up an automatic barrier between them. One that said hands off.

He often wondered whether, if he'd managed to make a move on her years before, he'd have had a chance with the girl of his dreams. If he'd only believed in himself enough to try. Didn't matter now. Even with his brother gone, having died in a car accident six months earlier, Keith was still between them. It was too late.

He shook himself out of his brooding about the past and focused on the woman at his door. "Maxie."

"Hi, Lucas." A flush stained her cheeks. Dark circles framed her eyes, and she had no makeup on her pretty face.

Realizing she was the subject of his scrutiny, she self-consciously pulled at a strand of blonde hair that had fallen from the messy knot on top of her head. She looked tired and fragile. She'd been through more than her fair share of shit with Keith, and Lucas sensed there was much he didn't know about their marriage and her life.

"Come on in," he said in the wake of her silence.

Twisting her hands in front of her, she walked past him into his apartment.

He shut the door behind her. "This way." He led her to the kitchen. "Can I get you a cup of coffee?" he asked, taking a long sip of his own. He sensed he was going to need it even more than he'd originally thought, because judging by her behavior, something was up.

"No. Thank you. I'm hopped up enough."

She didn't seem hopped up, but deflated. He knew she'd suffered from severe depression after losing the baby, but she'd seemed to be coming out of it lately and behaving more like herself.

He placed his cup down, grasped her hand, and led her into the den, where his wall-to-wall television and electronic sectional sofa were located.

Maxie was a year younger than him, and they'd been inseparable from the time his family had moved in to the Long Island neighborhood. Over time, the feelings he'd felt for her had become *more*, but he hadn't been the confident man he was today. He'd been the geeky younger brother who struggled with school, liked his video games, and wanted nothing more than to be in front of the computer screen. As opposed to his overachiever, sports-oriented older brother. Four years his senior, Keith was competitive to the extreme and thrived on Lucas' insecurities. Despite the lack of rivalry on Lucas' part, what Lucas had—or wanted—Keith had made it a point to take.

And that had included Maxie.

"What's wrong?" he asked her, knowing she wouldn't be here otherwise.

Although his brother had bought the apartment downstairs, another *fuck you* to Lucas that forced him to watch Keith with Maxie close up, he and Maxie had kept their distance after the marriage. And she'd pulled further away after losing the baby.

She opened her purse and pulled out a sheet of paper and handed it to him. The word FORECOSED jumped out at him, stamped on top.

His gaze shot to hers.

She nodded, tears in her eyes.

"I don't understand. Keith was a partner at a top New York law firm. He had to have left you well off. With insurance."

She shook her head, and he gave her a moment to compose herself. She finally met his gaze. "Your brother isn't... wasn't who you thought."

Lucas hadn't *thought* much of his older sibling, but that wasn't something he would share with his widow. It was enough he carried the guilt for the negative feelings he had for his dead sibling and the depth of emotion he felt for the man's wife.

"What do you mean?" Lucas asked.

She blew out a long breath, her brown eyes meeting his. "Most of it doesn't matter except for this. Keith was into gambling. Heavy-duty gambling, and I had no idea until after he died. He drained our accounts, took money from the 401-K, and hadn't paid any of the life insurance he had."

Lucas stiffened as he absorbed that information, but too much still didn't make sense. "Okay, but banks don't just foreclose. They give you warning."

Her sad eyes met his. "When we moved in here, Keith was doing very well at the firm. He told me we paid off the mortgage. Then, after he died, of course I didn't make any payments because I didn't think there were any to be made." She glanced away. "I had no idea Keith had taken out another mortgage and somehow forged my name until the sheriff delivered the notice!" she said with the first show of anger since she'd arrived.

Lucas glanced at the paper in his hand, still confused. If it had been a warning, he could have paid off the debt and saved her home. "Didn't you get advance notice? They usually give you time to make payments. I could have taken care of things."

She shook her head. "I called the bank. Apparently they had a post office box on file, not the house address. Keith hadn't paid the mortgage in almost a year. Here I thought at least I had the apartment free and clear, because thanks to the gambling, there was nothing left."

He stared in disbelief. "Why is this the first time I'm hearing about this?"

"Because I thought I could handle things." She shifted her gaze from his, her hands twisting in her lap. "I got a job for minimum wage at a boutique and—"

"Hold on." He held up one hand, interrupting her. "You're a paralegal at Keith's firm. What happened to your job?"

"The partners fired me after Keith died and the truth about him came out. He'd been siphoning money from the firm too. I'm tainted goods by extension. I can't get a job at another criminal law firm. Nobody will go near me. I have resumes with a lot of civil firms but no bites."

Shock rocked through him. Lucas had never had a good relationship with his sibling, and he knew damn well he'd been a shitty husband. It had taken everything in him to watch the sparkle leave Maxie's gaze over the last few years, but he'd told himself it wasn't his business. He'd had no idea Keith had been a thief and a gambler.

"If he were here, I'd strangle him," Lucas muttered.

"I've thought the same thing myself." She twirled a strand of hair around one finger nervously. "I've been paying the utility bills and buying food. You know, the basics, but I thought at least I had the apartment to my name."

His head was spinning with the amount of information he hadn't known, and he ran a hand through his hair. "Why am I just hearing about any of this? Obviously you know I'd help you, because you're here now," he said, unreasonably hurt she hadn't come to him when she'd realized she had no means of support.

She lifted her shoulders. "I spent years under Keith's thumb, letting him take care of things, and look where that got me. Why do you think I changed my name back to Sullivan? I want… need to stand on my own. And in this case, I didn't want to be a burden." She reached out and took his hand. "You'd have been there for me. You always are, but you don't need my problems in your life."

That hurt. As much as he understood her rationale, he had always wanted to be the person she could turn to. "You could never be a burden."

"I'm about to be one because I have nowhere to go. I had a friend I planned to move in with, and at the last minute, she changed her mind. She wants her boyfriend to move in instead."

"Some friend."

A small smile lifted her lips. Lips he couldn't tear his gaze away from, no matter how desperate her situation. Which made him a jerk.

"And I can't ask my mother for anything. We barely speak. I really do have nowhere to go." Her eyes shimmered with tears.

"Of course you do and you know it. You can stay here until we figure out your next step. I have three bedrooms. It'll be fine. You won't even be kicking me out of my home office."

She met his gaze, gratitude in her expression. "It won't be for long, I promise. Just until I figure a few things out. I told you I have resumes sent in to civil law firms. The partners at Keith's firm agreed to give me a letter of recommendation as long as I stay away from criminal law. I'm hoping to make a fresh start. If I live carefully, I can save and be out of here—"

"Maxie, stop. You'll stay here as long as you need," he said, refusing to think about what that close proximity between them would mean.

Of course, his cock immediately registered the fact and began to perk up. Sister-in-law, he harshly reminded himself. Grieving widow. Woman who'd suffered a severe loss. He had no right or intention of making a move on her.

"Thank you," she said on a shaky exhale. Without warning, she rose from her seat and threw her arms around his neck, hugging him tight.

He cradled her back, breathing in her familiar strawberry shampoo scent, and a sense of longing shot through him. The kind he'd pushed aside for years because he had no choice. She elicited emotions from deep inside him, and his body grew even harder at the feel of her soft curves in his arms.

He grasped her shoulders and separated them before she became aware of his reaction to her nearness. "It'll be okay," he said, taking in her glassy eyes.

"Thanks to you." She straightened her shoulders. "I really wanted to stand on my own two feet, but every time I turn around, another hit comes. There was so much Keith did behind my back…" She shook her head. "But it doesn't matter. Thank you for helping me. I hope it won't cramp your social life," she said, not meeting his gaze.

"I'm more than happy to share my video controllers," he said with a wink, hoping to lighten the mood.

The pathetic fact was, since canceling his date the night he'd come to her rescue, he hadn't been out with another woman.

She grinned and he breathed out a groan of relief.

"So you have thirty days to pack and get your belongings into storage before you have to be out?" he asked.

"A week. I thought I had somewhere to go, remember? I already have some things boxed."

"We'll finish up this weekend," he said.

"What do you mean, *we*? I can handle it," she assured him.

Did she really think he was going to leave her to handle everything alone? "Have you planned for storage or donation?"

She shook her head. "I was just focused on my things." She glanced down. "Your parents want Keith's things, so I figured I'd call them about storage."

He braced his hand around the tight muscles in the back of his neck. "I'll take care of it. By the time the weekend arrives, I'll have arranged for a unit for everything. I'll also contact Goodwill for a large pickup—"

"Lucas, I can do it." He heard the steel in her tone.

"I know you can. I want to help."

"Just this once." She let out what sounded like a relieved sigh, giving in. On such short notice, she had to really need the help.

"I meant what I said about standing on my own." A warm smile lifted her lips. "I don't know how to thank you."

He didn't want her thanks, but he could never have what he truly desired. "That's what family is for." He forced the words out of his mouth. The ones that created distance and reminded him of his place in her life.

She immediately jerked back and he knew he'd hurt her. "Right. Well, then, I should get going." She turned and headed for the door.

His gaze fell to the seductive sway of her hips as she walked out. Her body had filled out, become curvier, and his mouth watered at the sight. He shifted positions and readjusted his cock in his pants. Somehow he'd managed to ignore the fucker during Maxie's visit and subsequent conversation, but she'd gone and hugged him. And his body had reacted.

Which only served to reinforce how difficult his life was about to become.

MAXIE SOON DISCOVERED that, unlike his brother, Lucas was as good as his word. By the time Saturday rolled around, she had more boxes, tape, and everything she needed to help with the arduous work of packing up her house, sorting through what she could keep with her in his apartment, what she would put in storage, and what she chose to throw or give away.

She tagged the furniture she wanted to keep, and she marked other things for Goodwill. She was brutal with her decisions. For one thing, she didn't want any more reminders of her life with Keith than she had to have. And for another, she didn't care how much money Lucas had, she wasn't going to overfill storage units or ask him to pay for more than one for her things. Everything that was Keith's, she kept for his parents. Lucas said he'd be covering the storage costs, for which she was grateful.

She was keeping track of what she owed him, and she planned to pay back every penny. She wouldn't be beholden to another man ever again.

She was deep into box number ... she'd lost count when the doorbell rang. She answered, only to come face-to-face with Lucas and two other extremely handsome men who looked vaguely familiar. But no matter how good-looking they were, she only had eyes for Lucas.

He'd gotten a shorter haircut, and his face had a healthy dose of scruff, adding to his appeal. He wore a black tee shirt that accentuated muscles he hadn't possessed as a kid and a sleeve of tattoos that looked sexy as sin on his well-built body.

She was instantly aware of her messy updo, torn jeans, and makeup-free face, realizing she hadn't presented him with her best side lately. She shouldn't care. But she did.

"Lucas," she said, tucking a messy strand of hair behind her ear.

"Morning, sunshine. Ready to get yourself packed up?"

She stared, open-mouthed.

With a sexy grin, he reached out and eased her jaw shut. "I told you we'd start this weekend."

"I know and I've been at it for a couple of hours. I just didn't expect help."

He frowned at her. "And that's the problem."

Before she could reply, he gestured at his friends. "Maxie, meet Derek and Kade, my partners and best friends."

Which explained why they looked familiar. She'd seen them in the news with him.

"And I'm Lexie," a pretty brunette said, coming up behind them and pushing between the men. "Sorry. I was on the phone outside but I'm here now."

"Nice to meet you all." Overwhelmed, Maxie managed a smile. "Come on in."

The men took charge of the furniture, while she and Lexie headed to the bedroom. As they packed and worked, she learned more about how Lexie and Kade had met when she'd come to work for him as his personal assistant. Apparently Kade was a pain in the ass in the workplace, but Lexie had held her own with the man.

The other woman was warm, friendly, and brutally honest. About how much she loved her husband and how he'd been there for her when she had problems with her bipolar sister. Within an hour, Maxie felt a kinship with Lexie and wanted to get to know her even better.

Maxie also learned about the problem the men had had with an ex-friend and former business partner who had almost derailed the IPO by blackmailing Kade. And how he'd used her sister in the process. Maxie was in shock. She had no idea what they'd all gone through. Maybe because after she'd lost the baby, Keith had cut off all contact with his brother and insisted Maxie do the same.

With depression blanketing her, she'd barely been able to focus on herself, let alone friendships. When she'd been strong enough, Maxie had tried to leave Keith, but he'd held cards that prevented her from walking out. She'd unhappily stayed, knowing she was protecting Lucas in the process.

He didn't know and she didn't plan on enlightening him. He already hated his brother. With Keith gone, she didn't need to deepen the wounds.

"I assume you're taking everything in here with you?" Lexie asked loudly from the walk-in closet, where she was boxing shoes. One thing Maxie loved about this Manhattan apartment, it had amazing-sized closets.

Maxie nodded, then realized the other woman couldn't see. "Yes. Clothes, shoes, all going upstairs."

"What about this box?" Lexie stepped out of the closet with a large carton in her hand, and Maxie's breath caught in her throat.

Lexie held a box of baby things that Maxie had kept hidden from Keith. She should have been prepared; after all, it was never far from her mind, but the move had consumed her thoughts. A welcome distraction from the pain of loss. Keith had thrown out everything he could get his hands on in the days afterward, angry at Maxie for losing his son.

No matter what the doctor said, Keith had blamed her for doing too much. For not taking care of herself. He didn't want any reminders but she did. He'd had no idea she'd kept things with the most sentimental meaning.

Lexie had placed the box on the bed, and Maxie lifted the cardboard top, picking up a stuffed lamb and holding the soft fur to her cheek. The box also contained, among other things, a blue baby blanket with a satin edge and the crib mobile she'd fallen in love with when she'd gone shopping with her friends.

"Oh, I'm so sorry," Lexie said, walking up beside her. "I can't imagine what you've been through."

Maxie met her gaze. "Thank you. It's been… beyond painful." She gingerly placed the lamb back in the box. "Can you hand me some tape? I'm going to put this in storage," she said, forcing the words past her tight throat.

"Sure." Lexie handed her the packing dispenser.

The other woman respected her silence and obvious need to be alone with her thoughts, and for a little while, she and Lexie worked quietly, boxing up clothes and piling them into labeled boxes.

Maxie looked up from where she was kneeling on the floor. "I appreciate you spending your Saturday helping a stranger," she said, tired of the silence.

"Oh, I don't mind. I'm happy to be here. Besides, Lucas thinks the world of you. He wouldn't have rounded us all up to help otherwise."

Maxie's cheeks grew warm at the mention of Lucas' feelings. Probably because she knew how strongly she felt for him and how impossible a relationship between them still was.

"Lucas is a good man," Lexie went on.

"The best," Maxie agreed.

"Maxie?"

She jerked at the sound of her name and realized Lucas was standing in the doorway. From his tone and the pained look on his face, he'd obviously overheard her confession.

"I… umm…"

"I'm going to see if Kade needs help," Lexie said, jumping to her feet, clearly realizing they needed to talk. With an awkward glance at Maxie, Lexie slipped out of the room and Lucas strode in.

Suddenly the decent-sized bedroom felt smaller with just the two of them in it.

"You heard." She saw no point in beating around the bush.

"I did. And I'm glad you think so highly of me," he said with a sexy grin.

"Yes, well, don't let it go to your head, okay?"

"I'll try."

His smirk told her it already had.

"I just wanted to let you know the guys and I were going to take the furniture over to the storage unit. The Goodwill people will be here tomorrow with a truck to take everything else."

"Sounds good. Thank you."

He nodded. "By tomorrow everything will be up-stairs, and you can start unpacking. And by tomorrow we'll be living together."

She let out a long exhale and prayed for the strength to handle being under the same roof with the man she'd always desired... but could never have.

THE FIRST NIGHT in Lucas' apartment was an awk-ward one. They ordered in dinner and sat through a mostly silent meal of Chinese food, making small talk. Then she excused herself to start unpacking her bedroom and listened to him opening and closing drawers and taking a shower in the master bedroom next door.

She was acutely aware of his presence and couldn't stop imagining him lying naked in the king-sized bed she'd seen in his room. If she closed her eyes, she could envision his muscular body lying on top of the navy comforter, his sexy tattoos standing out against his skin.

She wanted to lick her way across his chest and down his arm, tracing the ink with her tongue. In her imagination she could taste the saltiness of his male flesh, and as a result she hadn't slept well, always conscious of her tingling skin, heavy breasts, and aroused body. It had been a long time since she'd experienced such strong sexual desire.

She woke up Monday after Lucas had left for work, and she spent the day organizing her new room. By the afternoon, she had time to sit down with her laptop and send out a few more resumes. Then she searched the kitchen cabinets and fridge for food so she could cook dinner. The least she could do in exchange for Lucas' generosity was find a way to earn her keep, and cooking for him made her feel useful.

Based on the contents of his refrigerator, he seemed like a basic-food kind of guy. She ran down to the grocery store to pick up a vegetable for dinner tonight, returned, and prepared the meal, planning to surprise him.

The surprise was on her, though, when Lucas didn't come home on time. She supposed she should have asked him his plans, but she'd just assumed he'd arrive around the same time she usually saw him returning from work when they ran into each other in the lobby.

She debated on whether or not to call him, but she didn't want him to feel obligated to her in any way. So she ate her dinner alone, cleaned up, put the leftovers in the refrigerator in case he hadn't eaten, and settled into the sofa.

She pulled out her laptop and began looking through her emails for the first time since this afternoon. To her surprise, she had an email from one of the places she'd submitted her resume.

She let out a squeal of excitement and immediately emailed them back to set up an interview. She began to do some Googling and reading up on the firm, taking notes on a pad she'd brought into the room with her. She was determined to bring her A-game. She needed this job. Needed it not just for the money and life's necessities but to prove to herself she was strong and capable on her own.

LUCAS' FIRST DAY of work after Maxie moved in, he couldn't bring himself to go home on time. Not after the night before, when they'd sat through a fucking awkward dinner and then he'd tossed and turned in his bed, knowing she was sleeping in the room next door.

The guest bathroom was outside the bedroom, and he'd caught sight of her walking toward it in a soft-looking tee shirt in light pink with lace trim. Her bare legs seemed to go on for miles, her silky hair falling over her shoulders in a sexy, tangled mess. And yeah, her nipples poked through the flimsy material, forcing him to jerk his head up and meet her gaze in order to not get caught staring.

He'd slammed the door to his room and hadn't come out for the rest of the night. He refused to think about what he'd done in the hours before dawn. With his hand. More than just once.

Shit.

"What are you still doing here?" Derek asked, stopping by his desk and taking a seat on the edge of it.

Lucas leaned back in his chair and stared up at the ceiling. Their office, located in a renovated garage in SoHo, was an open area on the main floor for the employees, with private offices above, each boasting wall-to-wall windows with a view that reminded him daily of how far they'd come.

"Avoiding going home," he said, honest with one of the men he trusted above all others.

"The pretty lady has you tied up in knots already?" Derek asked.

"She's had me tied up in knots my whole life."

A smirk lifted Derek's mouth. "Yeah, I know. So what are you going to do about it? You could always make a move," he suggested.

"On my brother's grieving widow?" The words felt raw and gritty in Lucas' mouth.

Derek raised a shoulder. "You so sure she's grieving?"

Lucas opened his mouth, then closed it again. "She married my brother."

"Everyone has reasons. Ever ask her hers?"

Lucas swallowed hard. "No."

"And on that happy note, I'm out of here." Derek pushed himself up and off the desk. "Learn from Kade. Women are either a pain in the ass or you can't live without them. Might as well figure out what yours is."

Lucas rolled up the nearest piece of paper and tossed it at Derek. "Go home." And he'd do the same.

Not to make a move on his houseguest but to begin living whatever his life was going to be like now.

A little while later, Lucas walked into his apartment to the delicious smell of dinner, reminding him he'd skipped a meal. He stopped at the kitchen, which was sparkling clean, and glanced in the refrigerator. A plate with a note for him to microwave dinner if he was hungry.

He was. But he wanted to thank her first.

He headed toward her bedroom and caught sight of her curled up on the sofa. He stepped closer. She had one hand beneath her head, her hair falling around the throw pillow and her lips slightly parted. The television scrolled movie credits in the background.

His heart kicked hard in his chest.

He knelt down and brushed her hair off her cheek. "Maxie."

"Hmm." Her nose twitched and she rolled over, her eyes opening wide. "Lucas."

He loved the sound of his name on her lips.

"You're home."

"Better late than never."

She pushed herself to an upright position and curled her legs beneath her. "There's dinner in the fridge. If you haven't eaten."

"You cooked?"

She nodded. "I figured it was the least I can do."

"Thank you. And I'm sorry I didn't make it home in time."

She lifted one shoulder. "It's fine. I'm used to eating alone. And I don't mean that in the pathetic sense. I did it long before Keith passed away."

She was independent and he respected that about her. But the innuendo behind the comment got him thinking. Maybe it was none of his business, but he couldn't help but be curious what her life had been like with her husband. And why she'd stayed with him to the end.

So he kicked off his shoes and sat back beside her. "Mind if I ask you a question?"

"Go for it," she said, meeting his gaze.

Chapter Two

"WAS IT ALWAYS like that? Your marriage, I mean."

Maxie thought she was prepared for a serious question, but she hadn't thought he'd dive into a conversation about Keith already. But she wasn't going to avoid the question.

"No. In the beginning things were good. I moved to Manhattan after graduation, and I ran into Keith one of the first nights here." Her eyes glazed over and she was clearly lost in thought. "I was out with friends and he was at the same restaurant. We talked, I told him I was looking for a job, and he offered to put in a word at his firm. He seemed so different from the pompous jerk he was when we were growing up. His firm hired me and we spent time together as friends. You were out in Silicon Valley then. And we'd lost touch for a while," she reminded him.

"Do you want a drink? A glass of wine?"

She thought about it and nodded. She might as well have some fortification for this talk.

"Red? White?"

"White is good."

"I have a nice Moscato chilling. I'll be right back."

She watched him go, her gaze drawn to his wide shoulders and trim waist. God, he was sexy, she thought, and so different than her computer-loving childhood friend. He was every inch a sexy man now, and she shifted in her seat, all too aware of her body's heated reaction to waking up and finding him staring into her eyes.

He returned a few minutes later and handed her a glass. She took a sip of the fruity drink and smiled, running her tongue over her lips, belatedly aware he'd catalogued the movement.

She treated herself to another, bigger taste.

"So. Back to your story?"

"Right." Her fingers curled tighter around the stem. "Keith and I started spending more time together at work, and after. The first few times he asked me out, I said no. I didn't want to mix business with pleasure."

And she'd still been holding out hope that Lucas would come home and maybe he'd finally see her in a different light. One that didn't keep her in the friend zone.

"I'm amazed he was able to be on his best behavior for so long."

"He was a very patient man when there was something he wanted," she said, having learned just how true that was.

"What made you change your mind and go out with him?" Lucas asked in a tight voice.

She placed her glass on a coaster on the end table. How much of the truth did she tell him? she wondered. Then realized it couldn't hurt to admit what had driven her into Keith's arms the first time. As long as she didn't sound like she was carrying a torch for Lucas all these years, she'd be fine.

"Well, every so often I'd ask him about you. Especially after seeing a picture of you in the paper or a mention online. One night I asked how you were doing. He told me you were engaged and… I guess it hurt to hear about it from someone else. I—"

He jerked and nearly spilled his wine. "Wait, did you say he told you I was *engaged*?" he asked, placing his wineglass beside hers.

She nodded. "I was happy for you—" And jealous, she silently admitted.

"I was never engaged," he said through clenched teeth.

She narrowed her gaze. "But I'd seen pictures of

you and a woman online—" Someone he was working alongside in California. Someone, she figured, he had a lot more in common with, as his business took off at such a young age, than he had with Maxie.

"Arielle? She was the CFO at a software company that was helping us get started. That's all."

Maxie shook her head. "But Keith said your parents told him the news."

And Maxie had been devastated. Unreasonably so because they really had drifted apart during their college years. But she'd been in love with him and that hadn't gone away. She'd held out hope for *one day*... until that night, anyway. Her hopes shattered, she'd soon after agreed to date Keith. After all, he'd been nothing but good to her. Her work friends and college friends were in serious relationships. A few had gotten engaged. She wouldn't say her biological clock was ticking, but she'd wanted more in her life. Was ready for a real relationship and a family sooner rather than later.

"I just assumed the engagement ended for whatever reason." And she'd already become heavily involved with Keith, and he'd kept her focus solely on him.

"I never even slept with her," Lucas muttered. "My brother lied." He clenched his fists so tightly his knuckles turned white.

Maxie tried to absorb the truth. With all she knew

now about her husband, she wasn't surprised he'd lied, but back then? He'd been the perfect gentleman, a good friend, a solid mentor at the office. He'd guided her in every aspect of her life… to exactly where he wanted her, she realized now.

"Oh my God." She put her head in her hands. "He manipulated me completely." Swept her off her feet in the guise of keeping her from pining for his brother.

Lucas grasped her wrists and pulled her arms away from her face, forcing her to meet his gaze. "It's not your fault. He was damned good at manipulation."

She blinked back tears. "Maybe, but I still not only fell for it but I let him use me to hurt you." She shook her head. "Or he thought he was hurting you. We'd drifted apart by then, so why in the world would he think you'd care who I dated… or married?"

His strong hands remained around her wrists, holding her in place. "You said you would ask about him about me, right?"

She nodded.

"I asked about you."

She sucked in a surprised breath. Well, maybe she shouldn't be so shocked. They'd shared enough longing looks since she'd moved into the building that told her he hadn't forgotten about her either. She just hadn't been aware of his interest at the time. Nor did she know if his questions had been friendship-based or a wish for something more. But considering she'd married his brother, the ultimate betrayal, did it really matter?

He leaned in, his forehead meeting hers. "Don't beat yourself up," he told her, his thumbs brushing over the pulse points in her wrists.

Her entire body responded to his touch. As his calloused fingertips skated over her skin, her nipples peaked and her sex grew heavy and moist. She inhaled and took in the fruity wine scent on his breath. Neither broke the moment, and their breathing grew more labored, in sync with each other.

"He's gone. He can't hurt you again," Lucas assured her.

But Maxie knew better. When it came to Keith, the blows kept coming.

"I need to get some sleep," she said, pulling back before he... or she could act on this thing between them. She didn't deny it existed, but she knew it was more powerful than anything she'd experienced before in her life.

She'd already put her faith in a sociopathic liar until she'd lost herself completely. She couldn't allow her need and desire for Lucas to override common sense and drag her back into relying on a man too much. Not even one as special as Lucas.

WHILE DEREK STOOD off to the side, Lucas beat the shit out of the heavy bag, trying not to envision his late brother's face as his target. Now that he knew how far Keith had gone to get Maxie to date him, he allowed the anger he'd held back to wash over him and pounded on the inanimate object until sweat poured down his body and some of the anger and frustration abated. He doubted he'd ever lose the feelings completely.

Engaged.

Keith had told Maxie Lucas was engaged to a woman he'd only had respect for and nothing more. There was no way in hell his parents had relayed any information about Lucas' personal life to Keith. Because Lucas never shared it with them. No, Keith had made up the story to get Maxie into his bed. And ultimately, it had worked. Lucas swung hard once more, connecting and feeling not just the reverberation through his arm and shoulder but the burn in his muscles.

"Okay, you've had enough," Derek said, waving a hand to get Lucas' attention.

He pulled back mid-punch and bent over, hands braced on his thighs as he pulled in much-needed air.

"Feel better?" Derek asked.

"Not sure," Lucas muttered.

Derek's smile was grim. "Let's grab a beer. Kade

might be too much of a pussy to leave his wife and join us, but we can have a drink and talk you down."

"Kade's got it good and you know it." Lucas pulled off the large gloves and hung them on the wall, then slowly unwrapped his hands.

"Yeah. Still want to get that drink?"

"I need to grab a shower first."

A little while later, they were seated in a small bar near the gym, each drinking a Highland Ale. "I still want to kill him," Lucas muttered, speaking of his brother.

"Unfortunately that's already done."

Lucas winced. "And that's what makes this so damned hard. I can't confront him. I can't get closure of any kind." He tipped the bottle back and took a sip of the malty brew.

"You're going to have to come to terms. Nothing else you can do." He pulled a sip too. "Did you talk to her about anything else? About the two of you?"

He shook his head. "Once she realized she'd been deceived, she was so thrown and upset, I couldn't. Truth is, she freaked out when we got close. I can't push her."

"At least you've got her under your roof. That'll buy you some time."

Lucas hoped so. "I'm going to head home." He threw money on the scarred bar to cover both tabs and a tip. "Thanks for working out with me tonight."

"Always," his best friend said.

A little while later, he walked into his quiet house and tossed his keys onto the pass-through near the kitchen.

As he walked toward the bedrooms, he heard the sound of the shower running. Great. Just what he didn't need, the vision of Maxie in a steam-filled bathroom, naked, water running over her bare flesh. He only had his imagination to go by, but he envisioned her standing under the spray, head tipped back, eyes closed, rivulets of water running over her full, rosy-tipped breasts.

He swallowed a groan and adjusted his cock, knowing he was torturing himself for no good reason. He walked to the big TV room and sat down, flicking on the big screen and letting the news flood the room. He was trying to immerse himself in anything but the woman under his roof when he looked down at the table in front of the sofa. Maxie had left her laptop open, a notepad beside it.

He'd be lying if he said he didn't read what was on the paper. A list of civil law firms and research notes. Apparently she wasn't relying on the resumes she already had out. He admired her tenacity.

He glanced at the paper. And wouldn't you know, he'd worked with one of them when he and his partners were starting out, needing legal advice. Which meant he could help her get a foot in the door. He had no doubt she'd hold her own in an interview and if she obtained the position. But he also knew how difficult it was to stand out on paper alone, especially since she had no direct experience in civil law.

He could help her along. Just enough to let her step in and shine. He couldn't bear to see her get shot down before she had a chance to even prove herself.

One phone call. A favor called in. The rest would be up to her.

A FEW DAYS later, Maxie returned to Lucas' apartment after a quick trip to the grocery store for ingredients to bake cookies. She remembered chocolate chip were Lucas' favorite, and she had time on her hands since the boutique had cut her hours because business was slow and she was the last hired. So what else did an unemployed woman do but make cookies?

She entered the lobby and ran into one of the older neighbors in the building who had always been lovely to her. "Hi, Mrs. Fielding, how are you and your husband doing?" Maxie asked.

"I'm fine but Mr. Fielding's acid reflux has been acting up," the white-haired woman said.

"I'm sorry to hear that. I hope you're cooking him

bland food?"

Mrs. Fielding smiled. "But of course. And how are you holding up?"

Maxie forced a smile. "I'm okay." It wasn't a secret that she'd moved from her apartment to her brother-in-law's, and Maxie had had to admit to financial difficulties when people asked why. And neighbors being neighbors, they did ask.

"I think it was very kind of your brother-in-law to help you out during your time of need."

"I agree," Maxie murmured. "I'm baking him cookies," she said, somewhat inanely, as she was uncomfortable with the conversation.

"You're a sweet girl. And at least you weren't living there when the place was broken into."

Maxie blinked, startled. "I'm sorry … what?"

"Oh! The note was under all our doors this afternoon. I guess you haven't seen yours yet. Apparently your old apartment was broken into. Mr. Potts found the place ransacked," she said of the head of maintenance for the building.

Maxie shivered. "Well, that's scary."

She nodded. "Keep your door locked. That's what we're doing. You can't be too careful these days."

For a building with a lock on the door, it was rare for someone to be able to walk in uninvited. Unless they followed another tenant inside. "Well, thanks for the heads-up. You be careful," she told the older woman.

"Thank you, dear. Talk to you soon."

"Bye," Maxie murmured. She headed up to Lucas' apartment as Mrs. Fielding strode out the door.

Maxie walked into the apartment and picked up the flyer slid beneath the door. She shook her head and left the notice for Lucas to see.

Then she settled in to bake. She'd just finished putting the tins in the oven and cleaning up the kitchen when her cell phone rang.

A number she didn't recognize popped up on the screen. "Hello?"

"Is this Maxie Sullivan?" a female voice asked.

"Yes?" She noticed a piece of cookie dough on her finger and quietly licked off the deliciousness.

"This is Andrea McDonnell from Power and Associates."

Maxie's stomach flipped in excitement. "Hi."

"We were very impressed with your resume and would like to interview you," the other woman said.

Maxie nearly dropped her phone. "That's wonderful. I'm completely flexible," she said.

"Well, we're eager to fill this position, so how about tomorrow at eleven a.m.?"

"Perfect." Her heart beat rapidly in her chest.

"Do you know where we're located?"

"I do." A quick glance at her notepad would give her all the information she needed.

"Then I look forward to meeting you."

"Same here," Maxie murmured.

After she disconnected the call, she let out a shriek of excitement and danced through the kitchen, her happiness tangible. She was ecstatic to hear back since she had not received a response to her email earlier. And something she hadn't felt in too long.

The cookie timer went off, interrupting her dance, and she grabbed a potholder, pulling the tins out of the oven and setting them on the counter. She turned the temperature off just as she heard the sound of keys in the door.

"Something smells incredible," Lucas said, his voice growing closer.

He entered the room, his big body filling up the kitchen despite its substantial size for a Manhattan apartment. She looked him over through lowered lashes. Though it was a workday, his wardrobe choice consisted of a pair of faded jeans and a black tee shirt with the Blink logo. He looked as delicious as her cookies, and she wanted to take a bite out of him.

Her thoughts stopped her in her tracks, and she felt her face flush. But his gaze was focused on the tin of treats, and he didn't notice her heated cheeks or her traitorous hormones. He walked over, picked up one hot, melty cookie, and devoured it in one bite.

"Mmm," he said, closing his eyes and swallowing with a satisfied groan.

Her girlie parts tingled. Yep, that's how she chose to think of them. If she got any more specific, she'd be blushing more and in deeper trouble than she already was.

"Good?" she managed to ask.

"Delicious. You're a woman of many talents," he said, the compliment warming her.

"Thank you."

A smear of chocolate sat on his lower lips. Unable and unwilling to stop herself, she stepped closer, reached out, and ran her finger over his mouth, transferring the chocolate from him to her.

She glanced at the gooey substance, hesitated a fraction of a second, and slid her finger into her mouth, licking off the remainder of the treat. Maybe it was her imagination, but she could swear she tasted Lucas on her tongue. She knew damn well she felt him low down in her sex. To hell with embarrassment, thanks to Lucas all she could do was feel.

His heavy-lidded gaze locked with hers. "Maxie," he said on a groan.

Her breasts tingled at the low rumble in his voice. Like the other night, she was playing with fire. But unlike the other night, she was feeling stronger and more in control. Just the fact that she had a job interview emboldened her and gave her strength, more like the Maxie Sullivan she'd been before Keith manipulated and warped her mind.

"Lucas." She whispered his name.

"Walk away," he said, his body taut and vibrating with what she knew was the same desire shooting through her veins.

"I can't."

His gaze darkened. "Then run before we do something *you'll* regret."

He hadn't said *we'll* regret it. He was worried about her.

"Or?" She wasn't sure where this bold Maxie was coming from, but she liked her. Had missed her.

"Or I'm going to pull you against me and kiss you. I'm going to taste that sexy mouth of yours, and while I'm doing it, you're going to feel exactly how much I want you. Will you run again then?"

"Oh God." He was laying it out for her, and she wanted everything he described. Craved it so much she thought she'd die if she deprived herself of the feel of his mouth devouring hers. The press of his hard, muscular body fitting to her curves. The thought alone had her heart racing.

She absently touched her tongue to her bottom lip, and when he traced the movement with his dark, dark eyes, she did the one thing she hadn't done in too long. Took something for herself just because she wanted it.

"Do it," she whispered, her tone daring and husky with desire.

He stepped closer, his gaze intent on hers, as if waiting for her to change her mind. That wouldn't happen. She needed this like she needed air to breathe.

He twisted his hand in her long hair, slowly pulling her toward him, giving her a chance to say no. The tug on her scalp provided an erotic pull that went straight to her sex, arousal twisting desperately inside her. He leaned in, his face hovering near hers, his warm breath that hinted of chocolate a tease of what was to come.

Her lifelong desire was about to come true, and her heart pounded harder in her chest. She memorized the moment. The way his dark lashes fluttered down, fanning over to the tops of his cheeks. The sharp inhale of his breath seconds before his lips settled on hers.

She tasted him and stopped thinking at all, no longer able to catalogue memories. Only able to *feel*. He slid his mouth over hers with a satisfied groan, letting her know that he, too, was taking what he'd wanted for so long. He kissed her hard, holding her in place with his hand twisting in her hair. Biting at her bottom lip before gliding his tongue over the sting in a soft caress. Her sex swelled, desire mounting.

She wrapped her arms around his neck, let her hands come to rest in his hair, tangling her fingers in the short strands. Finding something to anchor herself to as best she could. Because he wasn't gentle with her. He took her mouth with the pent-up passion of a starving man, and she gave back just as hungrily.

Her tongue tangled with his, and his body shuddered with need. She needed to be closer and pressed herself against him, her unbound breasts smashed against his chest, only two sheaths of cotton separating her from feeling him skin to skin.

He tipped her head farther back, kissing her more deeply, and her pussy began to pulse with desire. Beyond thought or reason, she hooked one leg around him, and her sex came into contact with his rock-hard thigh. And she moaned as a pleasurable wave of arousal swept over her.

His fingertips bit into the skin on her arm while the other hand pulled harder on her hair. Need shot through her as her hips rotated against the rough denim of his jeans.

"God yes," she moaned again, knowing she could come from this motion alone. It had been so long since she'd worried about pleasing herself, and Lucas pleased her so much. Just being in his arms, floating away on a cloud of desire, so close to—

"No." He abruptly released her, setting her away from him, his breathing coming in a rough, labored hitch.

A dull roar echoed in her ears, and all she could focus on was how needy she felt, how empty. That and the fact that he'd pushed her away.

She shook her head in a vain attempt to clear the fuzzy haze of desire still filling her. "Lucas?"

"I can't take advantage of you," he said, stepping back but looking as shaken up as she felt.

She'd be lying if she didn't admit to taking some small consolation from the fact that she'd had an overwhelming effect on him too.

"You wouldn't have been." She felt compelled to point out that she'd been a willing participant.

But she understood his point. They had to live together, at least for now. And she couldn't afford to get wrapped up in a man. Even if every inch of her body desired and wanted to be filled by him, she had to get her life in order.

Which reminded her... "I have a job interview tomorrow!" she said, grateful to have something else to focus on besides that kiss.

His gorgeous brown eyes lit up as he clearly welcomed the change of subject too. "That's fantastic. Where?"

"A firm called Power and Associates. The woman

who called said she was impressed by my resume." She beamed like an idiot but she didn't care. It was her first step toward independence, and she intended to cherish every second.

"Congratulations. I think that deserves a celebration."

"It does?" She thought about it and grinned. "It does."

"Guess what I have?" He reached into his pocket and pulled out two tickets.

"What are those?"

"Tickets to the sold-out Museum of Ice Cream. It's in the Meatpacking District," he said, mentioning a trendy part of Manhattan. "And these babies are impossible to get."

Her eyes opened wide. "I saw a news clip on it. That sounds like so much fun."

"Then what do you say we head over there and celebrate your interview?" he suggested, sounding proud of her.

"It's not the same thing as an actual job but—"

He reached out and placed his finger over her lips. "Hush."

She parted her lips and he yanked his hand away. Apparently he was going to play it cautious, and if she was smart and was looking out for her future, she'd do the same.

Chapter Three

THE MUSEUM OF Ice Cream wasn't a real museum. It was a selfie-oriented place to have fun, and it was jam-packed with people. Although Lucas would normally have taken Maxie to a fancy dinner to celebrate her job interview, he knew how hard these tickets were to come by, and he'd had a hunch she'd enjoy the limited-time exhibit. Plus, he'd nearly had to wrestle Kade for the two tickets left by one of their advertisers. He couldn't let them go to waste.

The tour began with a scoop of ice cream, which they both devoured quickly, and he ended up with brain freeze.

"I want to do the Sprinkle Pool," Maxie said as soon as they arrived and looked at the list of stops they could make inside the six-room building.

He laughed at her enthusiasm, glad to see her willing to let go. It'd been a long time since he allowed himself to do the same, and her enjoyment was infectious. He wasn't sure how he felt about stepping into ice cream sprinkles and feeling them between his toes, but if that's what she wanted, he was willing to give it a go.

"You sure?" He pointed to the crush of younger kids stomping around, although he had to admit there were a good share of adults, their age and older, joining them.

"We're here, aren't we? I want to experience everything."

So, Lucas thought, did he. With her.

Unfortunately, his better judgment had taken hold earlier, and he'd pushed her away before things could go any further. The kiss was the hottest thing he'd experienced in his lifetime. And though he'd been building it up in his mind over the years, he had to admit finally having her in his arms had exceeded all expectations. He could only imagine what the next step would be like, viewing her body in all its naked glory, touching her bare skin, and tasting her tempting flesh.

He was beginning to get worked up all over again, and since he'd spent the last hour trying to cool himself off, he knew he had to think about other things.

"Take off your shoes!" Maxie said, already leaning

down and unbuckling her sandals.

As it was a too-hot late September week in Manhattan, they were both in lightweight clothes and no socks, making the process of slipping off their shoes easier.

"Did you read that there are eleven thousand pounds of confetti-colored sprinkles in there?"

He was more focused on the signs around the pool. *Dip at your own risk* and *Caution: May cause spontaneous happiness*, something he was experiencing himself. Except he had a feeling it was more the company than the place.

Still, he secretly admitted feeling like a kid again. Even if the Sprinkle Pool was a large area of plastic beads and not real ice cream sprinkles. Lucas didn't know if he was relieved or not that the experience was diluted and no more than a kids' activity.

He followed Maxie into the cool plastic pellets that were slipperier than he'd anticipated. She took a step and laughed, the sound light and wrapping around his heart. She made her way forward, and her foot slipped out from under her. He grasped her waist, catching her before she fell on her ass.

"Thanks," she said, turning around, her eyes alight with laughter. The bottom half of her body brushed against his, causing a jolt of pleasure to which his body reacted.

Knowing they were surrounded by people, he had to refocus himself. "Let's move on to the next stop," he said, just as a toddler squealed and wrapped his hands around Lucas' khaki pants, leaving a chocolate handprint in his wake.

He disappeared and his mother ran off after him, shouting an apology back at Lucas but her mind on her speeding child. He grinned at the sight. Someday he wanted that for himself. A wife and children. A family that was stronger and more cohesive than his had been. One where one child wasn't favored over the other. Where bullying and teasing weren't tolerated.

He glanced at Maxie, whose gaze followed the little boy, and his focus shifted as he read her mind, assuming she was focused on her loss. But when she glanced back at him, she was still laughing, pointing at his hand-painted pants.

"What's next?" he asked, following her out of the pool and back toward their shoes, where they quickly put them on. If she wasn't thinking about the past, he wouldn't be the one to bring it up.

"I want to check out the Miracle Berry place," she said, doing the last strap on her sandal.

He'd read the information earlier and shuddered. "A pill to change my taste buds?" he asked.

"Are you afraid to eat a lemon sticking out of ice

cream? You don't think you'll really taste sweet not sour?"

He didn't feel like finding out. He shrugged, embarrassed. "I'd rather try something else."

She laughed. "Okay, chicken, there are helium balloons near the spun sugar. What about that?"

"Why not?"

She led him where she wanted to go. After they made silly helium noises with teenagers who thought it was all too funny to make sex sounds, he grabbed Maxie's hand and directed her toward the Willy Wonka–themed Chocolate Chamber.

They entered through a curtain of brown satin, music playing in the background. He glanced around and caught sight of a huge beanbag chair, diving into it before anyone else could take the seat and pulling Maxie down with him. Cocoa bean fragments intentionally littered the floor around them, and the scent was pure heaven. A chocolate-themed movie played on a screen on one of the walls.

She leaned back, arms spread wide, and smiled. "This is magical. Thank you."

"My pleasure."

"Good job grabbing this bag."

He grinned. "Video games honed my killer instincts." She laughed and punched him lightly on the arm. "Silly." Her smile faded as she met his gaze.

"Mind if I ask you something?"

He shook his head. "Of course not."

"I saw you look at me in a panic when that little boy grabbed your leg."

He winced. He'd hoped he'd been subtle.

"Do you think I'm still fragile?" She bit down on her lower lip. The same lip he'd tasted earlier, and it was all he could do not to groan and kiss her again.

But this was a serious conversation. One that was long overdue since, after the night at the hospital, Keith had made certain they were never alone again. At least, that was Lucas' take, since Maxie had avoided him like the plague… until his brother passed away. Despite her grief, she'd been less skittish around him after Keith was gone.

He grasped her hand gently. "No," he said, forcing his mind back to her question, which he knew was important. "I don't think you're fragile. I didn't think you were fragile then, either. You were just—"

"Broken," she said softly. "And guilt-ridden."

Her words surprised him. "Why in the world would you feel guilty? The doctor said there was nothing you could have done to change the outcome."

Her eyes shimmered with tears. "Your brother didn't believe that. He blamed me. He said I worked too hard, and if I hadn't been putting together the crib, there wouldn't have been physical stress on my body and—"

"Are you kidding me?" Lucas exploded, causing people around them to stop and stare, and Maxie jerked back at his harsh tone.

"He was wrong," Lucas said in a more modulated voice. He ran a hand through his hair, taking a minute to calm the fuck down.

She nodded in agreement, which went a long way toward chilling him out.

"I know that now," she said. "But right after, I was so lost and depressed, searching for answers, and that was a point Keith kept hammering home. That it was my fault. Added to the postpartum depression, I couldn't help but fall deeper into depression and guilt."

Lucas stared down at her hand, running a thumb over her silken skin. "My brother knew how to manipulate people's emotions and not in a good way."

She drew a deep breath. "He was angry. Angry that I lost the baby and that I turned to you that night."

Never mind that he hadn't been around, Lucas thought in disgust. But he'd figured that was part of the problem. He and his brother hadn't spoken since he'd seen Lucas at the hospital until one night when he'd been drunk and run into Lucas in the lobby. Keith had warned Lucas to stay the hell away from *his* wife.

"Did he take his anger out on you too?" His entire body stiffened at the thought.

"Not physically. Keith preferred mental abuse." She shuddered at the memory. "It built up gradually, his manipulation. At first things were good. Then he started coming home later, claiming he was at work. When I figured out the truth, I confronted him. He agreed to work on the marriage. Looking back, I think things spiraled after he fell into debt. His behavior became more erratic. And I was tied to him by then, first with work, then with the pregnancy."

Lucas inhaled, drawing a deep breath of chocolate, which served to remind him of where they were. Though they were sitting in a room full of noisy people, the world had shrunk to the two of them.

Oblivious, Maxie continued. "After that night, when he didn't show up until the morning, reeking of booze and other women... I told him I was done. Leaving him."

Lucas' entire body froze. "What happened?"

Her tongue darted out, moistening her lips. "He said all it would take was a whisper or two in the right ears to let the SEC think there were violations going on at Blink. That he could derail the IPO and ruin you with one phone call." Her fingers dug into his skin as she revealed yet another despicable layer to his brother.

"That bastard." Every time Lucas didn't think things could get worse, another bombshell dropped. "And you believed him."

She lifted one shoulder. "I had no reason not to."

So Maxie had stayed in a miserable, emotionally abusive marriage because she'd been protecting him.

And didn't that make him feel good.

LUCAS ARRIVED AT the office bleary-eyed and exhausted, something that was obvious when Tessa, his assistant, walked into the room and handed him a cup of steaming-hot black coffee.

"Drink it," she said. "It might help get rid of those dark circles under your eyes." Her whole tone and demeanor were too perky for this hour of the morning.

Smartly, she read his mood and disappeared, leaving him alone. But she had a point. It was after nine a.m., and he should be more alert and functioning.

Unfortunately, he hadn't gotten much sleep the night before. Not after learning his brother had emotionally stripped Maxie bare and blamed her for the tragic loss of their baby. Not after he'd discovered Keith's threat to ruin Lucas if Maxie left him.

Lucas stared at the wall across from his desk, to the large photo on the wall of Lucas, Derek, and Kade, ringing the bell on the New York Stock Exchange. A crowning achievement for three nerdy kids who'd never fit in until they found each other. It wasn't bad enough that Lucas had been bullied and picked on by other kids, he hadn't even had home as an escape. No, he had Keith waiting to do more damage. Was it any wonder he lost himself in computer games where he could vanquish the bad guys and come out on top?

He wished he could focus on the positive today and not things he couldn't change. But he was preoccupied with the past. And it killed Lucas that his brother had manipulated and hurt Maxie. That he and Maxie had lost years of friendship, if not the chance for something more, due to Keith's blatant lies. But it was more than lost time that bothered Lucas now. It was the way his older sibling had played them. And he was continuing to play Lucas from the grave.

And he was allowing it. As long as he didn't take what he wanted with Maxie, Keith was still getting what he wanted.

Frustrated his brother was gone and he had nobody to confront, Lucas shoved everything off his desk with a furious roar.

"If it wasn't nine in the morning, I'd have a fucking drink," he said out loud in the empty room.

"And I'd pour you one." Derek stepped inside the office and closed the door behind him. "At least you didn't hit a wall like Kade did when he was having issues. What's going on? Problems with Maxie?"

"Problems with my dead bastard brother. How's that for a heap of guilt and anger I can't get rid of?"

"Guilt?" Derek asked, sounding incredulous. "Why? Because you hate the bastard? Look, I understand it isn't easy to hate a sibling, let alone one who died young, but Keith made your life a living hell often and for no reason other than jealousy. I'd let the guilt go."

Lucas braced his hand on the back of his neck and stretched from side to side. "It's hard when my mother's still crying over her son."

They both remained silent for a moment while that sobering thought sank in.

"Maybe you do need a drink," Derek said. "What happened to bring all this up again?"

He gave his friend a quick summary of last night's conversation.

"What the fuck are you waiting for?" Derek asked. "You feel something for this woman, still. After all these years."

"I can't deny that." And that was part of what had kept Lucas up all night—his pulling back from that kiss when he'd wanted so much more.

When she'd wanted more.

"So do something about it." Derek leaned down

and picked up some of the books Lucas had shoved to the floor, tossing them onto the desk.

"I intend to. I just can't overwhelm her. I can't move in like my brother did and take over."

"Which I know you want to do. Did you put a word in with that law firm?"

Lucas had confided in Derek about his intention to ask them to move Maxie's resume to the top of the heap. "I did."

Derek laughed and slapped him on the back. "Way not to take over, man."

Lucas picked up the stray papers he'd tossed, grateful for something to do to keep busy. "I just made it possible for her to be interviewed. Her resume won't get lost in the shuffle. That's all."

Derek nodded. "I hear you. I'd have done the same thing in your shoes."

It had taken all Lucas' self-control not to remind the head partner of the law firm just how much money Blink had made them and demand they hire her. He was proud of himself for his restraint.

But when it came to pursuing her—and he damn well intended to—he'd have to rein in the impulse to take what he'd wanted for what seemed like forever. To make Maxie his in all ways.

Last night she'd made it clear that she wasn't fragile and didn't want him to consider her that way. He would take those words to heart and step up his game.

He hoped she was ready. Because Lucas intended to get his girl.

MAXIE WALKED INTO Power and Associates, nearly choking on nerves. She was grateful for the interview and didn't want to blow it. She'd prepped by studying the firm's history. Elliot Power had started the firm and brought his son in with him. She'd looked into current clients and the types of civil cases they'd handled, wanting to be knowledgeable. Although this was a civil law firm and she'd specialized in criminal, she was a fast learner, and she knew she could handle things. Or so she assured herself as she walked up to the receptionist.

"Hi. My name is Maxie Sullivan. I have an interview with Andrea McDonnell at eleven."

"One minute."

The dark-haired woman picked up the phone while Maxie looked around. The office looked modern, a lot of black and white with sleek lines and photographs of ad campaigns surrounding her.

"Ms. Sullivan?"

"Yes?" She turned back around. "Ms. McDonnell will see you now."

"Thank you." Maxie followed the younger woman

down a hallway and into an office.

"Come in," an attractive redhead said, rising from behind her desk.

Maxie stepped inside and shook the woman's hand. She settled into a chair across from her and began the typical interview process. Maxie's palms sweat, but she did think she held her own on the *why do you want to work here* type questions, and the more esoteric, *where do you see yourself in five years*. The conversation shifted, and the subject of sororities in college came up, at which point they discovered they were sisters at different schools, and Maxie liked the other woman.

They sat for an hour after the initial questioning, talking about the job and the responsibilities, and Maxie asked her fair share of questions too. To her surprise, Andrea went over the salary, a little less than what she'd been making at her old law firm but more than livable, health benefits, and a 401(k). She'd be lucky to land this job after her first interview, she thought, her stomach twisting in anticipation.

"Well, I appreciate you coming in on such short notice," Andrea, as she'd asked to be called, said to Maxie.

"My pleasure." She brushed her hand down the front of her skirt and rose from her seat. All in all, she felt the interview had gone well. Now the nerve-racking job of waiting began. "Thanks for your time," Maxie said and started for the door.

"Maxie, wait."

"Yes?" She turned around and waited.

Andrea rose to her feet. "As I told you on the phone, we'd like to fill this position quickly. And we've seen a few excellent candidates."

Maxie's stomach fell as she anticipated the worst. "I understand." It normally took many interviews and a lot of pounding the pavement to wind up with a new job.

Andrea tipped her head. "I hope so because none were as perfect of a fit as you." She extended her hand, and numb, thanks to her shock, Maxie shook it. "Consider yourself hired."

"Really?" she couldn't help but ask.

"Truly," she said with a wink.

"Oh my God. Thank you!" She couldn't conceal her excitement and Andrea grinned. "Welcome aboard. Why don't you take the day tomorrow, get your things in order, and you can start on Wednesday, if that works for you?"

"Yes. Yes, it does." It was all she could do not to tap her feet and twirl around the woman's office. She'd done it, her interview sealing the deal.

"Let me walk you out," Andrea said, smiling.

"Thanks." They started for the door, and as they

rounded the corner that led to the front desk, a man called out, "Andrea!"

The other woman turned.

"Is this—"

"Maxie Sullivan, our new paralegal," Andrea said before the man, who Maxie recognized as the company owner, could finish.

"Maxie, meet Nick Power."

"It's nice to meet you," she said.

He shook her hand. "Everything work out okay?" he asked Andrea.

"Perfect. I can see why Lucas Monroe asked you to take a look at her resume," Andrea said.

Nick Power winced and Maxie's stomach sank in disappointment.

"He only asked us to put your resume on top of the pile," Nick said, trying to smooth things over.

"It's fine," Maxie said, absorbing the realization that Lucas had called in a favor to get her this job. One that was supposed to remain secret.

The high from acquiring the job deflated, leaving her feeling hollow. Still, she needed this job and all the perks that came with it. The salary and the benefits. "I'm grateful for the job, Mr. Power."

"Nick," he insisted. "We're very informal around here. And make no mistake, Andrea wouldn't have hired you unless you were qualified."

Maxie glanced at Andrea, who appeared uncomfortable with her slip of the tongue.

"Well, thank you both. I'll see you on Wednesday." She turned and rushed out, needing to deal with everything that had happened today and the emotions filling her in private.

Except she couldn't go home, because it was Lucas' home and she was upset with him. Not for trying to help but for doing it behind her back. If he'd asked, she'd have told him to keep out of it, that even if it took her months, she wanted to land a job on her own. Without a man pulling the strings.

Especially a Monroe brother. Because apparently, Lucas wasn't as different from his brother as he liked to claim. When given the chance, he stepped in and made things happen. So much for standing on her own, she thought, her anger growing.

And she was in no way ready to deal with him now.

Chapter Four

B Y SEVEN P.M., Maxie hadn't come home, and Lucas was starting to get concerned. She didn't have a job where she was running late; she'd had an interview earlier in the day. And he hadn't heard from her to know how the process had gone. They hadn't been living under one roof for long, but it wasn't like her to disappear without a word.

He'd called. He'd sent her a text. Or two. No answer.

He walked over to the window overlooking the city and stared down at the myriad lights shining, wondering where the hell she was. What if she was on a date with another man? How would he handle the fact that just when he'd decided to make a move, he was too late?

He clenched his hands into fists at the idea, his gut twisting with jealousy over something that hadn't happened yet. As far as he knew. But just the thought of some guy's hands on her in any way set his inner caveman loose.

When he finally heard a key in the lock, relief rushed through him. "Maxie?" he called out.

She passed by the family room and headed straight for her room, not answering him.

"Maxie?" he said again.

She turned, arms folded over her chest, and damned if his gaze wasn't drawn to the soft mounds beneath the silk blouse.

"Yes?" she bit out.

He narrowed his gaze at her angry tone. "You're late. I was worried."

"I was with a friend." She didn't elaborate, and irrational jealousy swung through him again.

"Were you on a date?" The word tasted gritty on his tongue.

She lifted one shoulder in a half shrug. "It would be none of your business if I was. Now, it's been a long day. Do you mind if I get some sleep?" She turned toward her room.

"After you tell me what's bugging you." He caught up with her in the hall and stopped her with a hand on her shoulder. "Did the interview not go well?" he asked, though he couldn't imagine her blowing it. She was smart and savvy and presented herself well.

"It went great. Perfectly, in fact, which I'm sure you already know since your friend, Nick Power, probably reported back to you."

He winced, finally understanding what was upsetting her. "I only—"

"Stuck your nose in where it didn't belong." Hurt and anger flashed in her eyes.

"Gave you a foot in the door," he countered. "Whatever happened after that was all you."

"Dammit, Lucas. Don't you understand what your brother did to me? He manipulated me into taking a job with him." She raised one finger in the air. "He got me to date him by telling me you were engaged." She added a second finger to the first. "He kept me with him by threatening someone I care about." A third finger raised. "And that's just a few of the things he did to control me. I need to make things happen for *myself*. And I told you that. The last thing I need is you pulling strings behind my back too. It makes you no better than Keith."

Her words hit him like an emotional blow as she pushed past him and stormed into her room.

Shit.

He'd never thought about one simple phone call that way. Helping her? Yes. Giving her a leg up? Definitely. But to have her lump his behavior with his brother's sat like lead in his stomach.

"Maxie." He pushed her door open and walked inside, needing to explain. She stood by the nightstand next to the bed, removing her necklace.

"I just wanted you to have the opportunity to meet with them. I never once thought I was undermining or manipulating you."

She turned to him, frustration in her eyes. "Well, you did both. And now I'll never know if I got that job on my own merit or because tech mogul Lucas Monroe called in a favor."

"I get it." He held up both hands in defeat. "So what are you going to do if they offer you the job?"

"They already did. The salary is good, benefits solid. I accepted, of course. I'd be stupid not to, no matter how it came to pass." She sounded sad when she ought to be excited and happy.

"I'm sorry, Max." He stepped closer, wanting her to forgive him as much as he wanted *her.*

"Well, that's something Keith never gave me," she murmured, her shoulders dropping in obvious relief. "Thank you. But Lucas, I need to grow and stand on my own, and I need *you* to respect that from here on out." She eyed him warily. "Can you promise me that?"

"Cross my heart," he said, meaning it. He'd do anything to put and keep a smile on her face.

Anything to have her in his arms.

"Maxie?"

"Yes?" She removed her earrings next, placing them in a tray on the nightstand, and met his gaze.

"Where were you all day?" And night. He asked the question that had been plaguing him all evening.

"My girlfriend Bailey's," she said, her lips twisting in a wry grin. "She's an artist. She paints and works from home. I hadn't seen her in a while, and I showed up with ice cream and we hung out all afternoon. Then we went out for dinner."

He exhaled a breath he hadn't known he'd been holding. "So you weren't on a date tonight," he said, aware of the relief in his voice and not giving a shit that he was putting his emotions out there for her to see.

"Not in the way you mean. Why do you care?" She met his gaze, all but daring him to answer.

Something he had no problem doing. "Because I *care* about you."

"I care about you too."

He wasn't talking about friendship anymore, and she needed to understand where he stood. Two steps and he was in her space, crowding her between the bed and the nightstand.

Her fruity scent was stronger in the bedroom and went straight to his cock. The time for pussyfooting around had come to an end. "I want you."

She blinked, her eyes alight with surprise. She obviously hadn't expected him to verbalize what had been unsaid for years. She hadn't anticipated him crossing the line between friends. But this morning he'd realized he couldn't maintain the status quo.

And tonight, pacing the floor, waiting for her to come home, he'd nearly lost his damned mind.

"Lucas—"

"Shh." He placed a finger over lips so soft, desire threaded through his veins. "I heard everything you said tonight and I respect it. I'll play by your rules, but fuck, Maxie, I *crave* you. Your touch, your taste, your body."

Her chocolate eyes darkened with a need that rivaled his. He wrapped a hand around her neck, pulling her close. "Say no." Because that was the only thing that would stop him from taking her mouth with his.

"Yes."

The word released all the frustration tonight had caused and the pent-up desire he'd been holding back for too long, and he slammed his mouth down hard on hers. She moaned and parted her lips, letting him inside. He took full advantage, devouring the deep recesses of her mouth, savoring her taste.

She moaned and pressed her breasts against his chest, the feel of those luscious mounds nearly causing him to lose it completely. He slid his mouth back and forth over hers, nipping at her lower lip, causing her to shudder and dig her nails into his shoulders. His dick pulsed inside his jeans.

He reminded himself to take it slow, but his heart pounded, and need beat a rapid pulse inside his chest. He tugged at the binding in her hair, and it spilled down, tumbling over his hands. He wanted to feel those strands on his bare chest and on his thighs as she took his cock into his mouth.

Slow, he reminded himself. Give her time to adjust to the idea of them. But nothing inside him allowed for slow. He continued to kiss her, as he turned and backed her against the bed. Her legs hit the mattress and she collapsed, taking him with her onto the bed.

She pulled at his shirt, sliding her hands along his sides and ribs. "Your skin is so hot," she murmured. "So tight."

He returned the favor, lifting her top and gliding his thumbs along her silken flesh. "And you're so soft." He pushed her shirt up and bared her stomach, pressing a kiss to her belly, sliding his tongue over her skin. She tasted a hint salty, and he continued a trail of damp kisses along her rib cage.

A loud banging noise sounded, and he jumped, ignoring it only to hear it again.

"Door," he said with a groan and rolled to his side.

"Who could be here at this hour?" she asked, immediately fixing herself, smoothing her hair and adjusting her clothes.

"Good question," he muttered, pissed at the interruption. "I'll get it."

He jumped up from the bed, adjusting his own clothes as he made his way to the door, cursing whomever had interrupted them.

LUCAS LOOKED THROUGH the peephole, uttering a curse when he saw his parents on the other side.

He glanced back toward the bedrooms, where Maxie was no doubt making sure she didn't look well-kissed and almost-fucked. He could not believe his parents' bad timing.

Or that they were here at all.

"Be right there," he called out, buying himself a minute to prepare.

Lucas hadn't told his parents that their daughter-in-law was living with him. He wouldn't say his parents favored Keith, but they had put him on a pedestal, and they didn't want him to fall from grace. Explaining Maxie's presence here would involve detailing even more of Keith's indiscretions and lapses in judgment.

And both parents were having a hard enough time accepting that their golden child had done anything wrong. Early on, Lucas had tried to broach the subject, explaining Keith's drinking and womanizing. His mother had cried and his father had cut him off, refusing to discuss the matter. Denial was a good way of describing how his parents were coping. Unless Maxie had told them, they didn't know about the embezzling or gambling, and he doubted she had.

Drawing a deep breath, Lucas straightened his shoulders and opened the door. "Mom, Dad. What brings you by?"

"Your father took me for dinner in the city. How could we not surprise our boy?" Justine Monroe said, pulling him into a hug.

His father, Bryce, nodded. "What can I say? She wanted it to be a surprise," he said, obviously more aware that they'd just dropped in unexpectedly.

Lucas shut the door behind them and led them into the area between the entry and the family room.

His mother had had a painful, difficult time since Keith passed away, becoming more reclusive at home, so he was glad she'd been willing to take a trip from Long Island for dinner.

He still wished they'd have called first, so he and Maxie could have prepared for the visit and discussed how to explain things. His parents knew about Lucas' old feelings for his brother's wife, and as a result, he didn't think they were going to take the news that she was living here well. At all.

"You look great, Mom."

"Thank you," she said with a smile.

Although she had more defined lines since Keith's death, especially around her eyes, she'd finally begun to have her hair colored red again. She was taking care of herself, and her full face of makeup attested to that fact, and it made Lucas happy.

"I'm glad you came in for a nice dinner," Lucas said, speaking loudly, hoping to prepare Maxie for the shock. It was up to her whether to come out or remain hidden in the room, opting to tell them another time.

"We had a delicious meal in the theater district. I told your mother we should see a show one Saturday night," his father said.

"A show sounds like a good idea," Lucas said, noting that his father, too, had changed recently.

His hair had been jet-black like Lucas' but was now grayer, his face also more lined. But they seemed to be slowly moving forward.

He hoped what they discovered today didn't cause a setback or a family rift.

"Hello, Justine, Bryce." Maxie walked out from the hallway where the bedrooms were and came up beside him.

She'd changed into a pair of jeans and a tee shirt and had washed her face and tied her hair back in a ponytail. There were no signs of the disheveled woman he'd kissed so thoroughly.

"Maxie?" his mother said, obviously stunned. "What are you doing here?" she asked, looking from her daughter-in-law back to Lucas.

"She lives downstairs. It's obvious she's here visiting," Bryce said.

"But she's coming from the bedrooms." His mother's forehead creased in confusion.

"Or the restroom. For God's sake, Justine, stop looking for trouble or creating drama."

"Mom, Dad—" Lucas began.

But Maxie stepped forward, taking control, and as he'd promised just a short while ago, he had no choice but to let her.

"The bank foreclosed on my apartment, and I had nowhere to go. Lucas was gracious enough to let me stay here until I get back on my feet," she explained, glancing at Lucas from beneath her thick lashes.

His mother's eyes opened wide. "But… but… I'm sure Keith had life insurance. He wouldn't leave you with nothing—"

"Mom," Lucas said, more forcefully than he'd have liked. "I tried to explain things about Keith to you a while ago, but you didn't want to hear." He drew a deep breath and dove in. "Keith lost everything. He died in debt. Maxie found out after he passed away, and she didn't know about the apartment until it was already foreclosed on."

"But… but…"

"Justine, come sit down," Maxie said, shooting Lucas a pained look.

Which left him to handle his father, whose expression went from stoic to crumbling, his posture suddenly hunched over. "Dad, let's go get a drink." Lucas led him to the kitchen while the women settled in the family room.

He poured two shots of whiskey and handed one to his father before downing one himself. "Dad, I'm sorry."

"About your brother? I am too. You're right. I didn't want to hear it. I still don't, but I can't ignore the fact that he left his wife destitute," he said, his voice rising.

"Here. Have another drink." He poured his father a final shot.

His father accepted it with shaking hands. "But as for Maxie, you can't mean to live here with her, Lucas. You just can't."

And here it comes, Lucas thought.

"She has nowhere to go, and I'm not throwing her out on the street."

"She can come live with us."

"She has a job in Manhattan. It's easier for her to live in the city than to commute from as far out on the island as you are. Besides, Dad, she barely wants to be here. She hates leaning on anyone. She's not going to want to burden you or Mom." Not that Lucas would let her leave here. "She's settled and it's fine."

"Of course it's fine for you. You've always been in love with her, but she's your brother's wife."

"Widow, Dad. And Keith did not do right by her. At all. I'm not saying there's anything happening between us, but if something ever did, it's none of your business."

"Whatever he did, Keith was still your brother, and you owe him some respect. That's his wife," his father said again.

Lucas leaned against the granite counter, his hands clenched in frustration at his sides. "Someday, I will explain to you exactly who your son was, and you'll listen and understand. Or maybe you'll choose to go on seeing him as he never was. A saint who could do no wrong. But if you do that, you'll lose me too. Because I can't live my life in denial like you are."

The words came out strong, but they hurt, and Lucas feared his father wouldn't listen.

"Justine!" Bryce called out, his face red with anger. He pushed past Lucas and stormed out. "Let's go!" he yelled for his wife.

A white haze of disbelief settled over Lucas as Bryce didn't even struggle to accept what his other son had told him. Grief, Lucas tried to remind himself. Bryce was grieving, and he couldn't cope with the facts. But the sad truth was, he hadn't seen who Keith had been even when he was alive. Not as a child and not as a man.

Lucas ran a hand over the top of his head and slowly made his way out of the kitchen and back to his parents, who were already at the front door. His father was rushing his mother out.

"Lucas—"

"Go, Mom. We'll talk when everyone's calm."

He glanced at Maxie, who was pale and shaken.

"But—"

"Justine!" Bryce barked out.

"It's okay," he mouthed to his mother. At least she wasn't as furious as his father. That gave him hope for the future.

Not, he thought, that he'd change his life to suit what his parents thought was right. Especially when it came to Maxie.

BY THE TIME Lucas' parents left, Maxie was shaking. She headed straight for her bedroom and pulled out the suitcase from beneath the bed and began throwing clothing into it.

"What the hell are you doing?" Lucas strode in and

slammed the top shut, leaving her holding a handful of underwear.

"I can't stay here." His parents were too upset, and she couldn't handle being the cause.

Lucas took the clothes out of her hands and laid them on the bed, neither mentioning that it was her panties he was holding.

He grasped her now free hand. "We didn't do anything wrong. I'm helping you out. Once they calm down and get over what they learned about Keith, they'll refocus their disappointment where it belongs."

She narrowed her gaze. "You don't really believe that."

A sad smile lifted his lips. Lips she'd been kissing not thirty minutes before. Her body tingled all over again.

"I don't care what they're thinking or how they're really coping; we're adults. They can't influence what we do," he said.

That's where he was wrong. "They were my in-laws, and they've always been good to me. And they're your parents. I don't want them hurting, and I won't be the cause of a rift between you."

He frowned. "And they don't want you suffering, regardless of how they reacted tonight. So you aren't moving out. Just take a deep breath and get some sleep. Give them some time to deal with things."

She blew out a slow breath, knowing he had a point. She had nowhere else to go anyway, which was why she was living here now. "I overreacted."

"No, you've just been through a lot."

She nodded. "So have you."

"I'd like to think we're out the other side and on our way to better things."

She smiled, appreciating his optimism. "I should get some sleep," she said, well aware if he remained in the room, talk would turn to what they'd been doing before his parents' surprise visit. And if they talked about it, she wasn't sure she could stop herself from repeating it.

And if his family was against her merely living here, she didn't want to imagine their reaction to her and Lucas being involved in any way. Despite what her body wanted, and there was no doubt she wanted Lucas, it wasn't a good idea for them to pick up where they'd left off. Now, as before, the timing wasn't right for them.

She was beginning to think it never would be.

MAXIE THREW HERSELF into work, determined to prove to her new employers that they'd made the right decision in hiring her. She didn't want anyone to think that she didn't pull her weight or that she had it easy just because Lucas Monroe had made a phone call. She made it a point to get in early in the morning and stay later than most in the evenings. Civil litigation was far different than criminal law, and she worked hard to learn fast and fit in. She enjoyed the work and the people and felt comfortable there.

Over the last week and a half, she and Lucas had settled into a routine. Since he had to pass her office on the way to his place of business, he insisted on giving her a ride to and from work. She, in turn, took care of cooking because it was something she enjoyed. He would clean up.

And to keep things simple, they retreated to their separate rooms after the meal ended. Sometimes she'd hear him watching television in the family room, but she chose not to join him. Instead she'd read in her bed and unwind from the day.

There had been a few awkward moments, like the time she'd woken up in the middle of the night and walked into the kitchen, wearing nothing but a tank top and panties, so she could get a drink. At three in the morning, she hadn't thought she'd need to cover up, but apparently Lucas had had the same idea. He'd walked in covered by nothing but a pair of tight boxer briefs, giving her a good outline of what was under-neath. The second he'd caught sight of her barely there outfit, he'd gotten hard. And Maxie got a glimpse of just how big and thick he was.

She hadn't been subtle about staring either. How could she have been when his erection was growing before her eyes? She'd wanted nothing more than to climb him, wrap her legs around his waist, and feel that masculine hardness against her sex. Her panties had grown damp, and she'd forgotten all about the drink, leaving it on the counter and escaping to her room before she could act on her desire. She'd returned to her room, slipped her hands beneath her panties, and rubbed herself to a nice, fast orgasm, thoughts of Lucas and what that erection would feel like inside her getting her off in seconds. She wouldn't be surprised if he'd done the same to himself in the room next door.

Neither of them had mentioned the incident the next day, but it was never far from her mind, and keeping her gaze on his face and not his... package wasn't easy. It had been a long time since she'd had sex. Since long before losing the baby, in fact, as Keith had lost interest in anything but his extracurricular activities. She'd thrown herself into the idea of becoming a mother and shut off all thoughts of intimacy and physical need.

Since moving in with Lucas, those needs had come roaring back to life, reminding her she was a woman. And this woman very much wanted the man she was living with. He should be off-limits but her body wasn't listening. From the often heated, slumberous look in his eyes when he looked at her, she knew he felt the same way.

Together they were smoldering embers waiting to be set aflame.

Chapter Five

L UCAS HATED BLACK-TIE affairs. All three partners at Blink did, which was why they alternated attending the ones that they deemed mandatory. For personal reasons, Kade took the events that focused on mental health issues, and Blink donated a lot of money there. Tonight Lucas was attending the Life Counts Gala, an event that raised money for suicide prevention among teens. Especially teens who were bullied. For obvious reasons, the cause was close to his heart, and Lucas did more than just donate money or attend a gala once a year.

With his first million, Lucas had immediately set about searching for a school system where he could help kids in need. No, he couldn't stop bullying on his own, but he could spend time with geeky kids like he'd been, children who loved math and computers and couldn't relate to the jocks and athletes who were more popular. Like his brother had been.

Lucas donated computers and iPads, knowing that geeks like he'd been would appreciate the technology they wouldn't have access to otherwise. These kids took one look at Lucas, who donated his time, saw his muscles and tattoos and his willingness to accept them for who they were, and it gave them hope that they, too, would survive adolescence. He loved giving them something to focus on, where they could learn to code, create, and get lost in their own worlds. Often a safer world than the one in which they lived.

He swore to himself that when he had a family of his own, no child of his would suffer at the hands of a sibling or feel as alone as he often had as a kid. So tonight's gala meant something special, and for that, he'd wear a tuxedo.

He adjusted his bow tie and shrugged on his jacket, grabbing his wallet and shoving it in his pocket before walking out of his bedroom.

To his surprise, Maxie sat on the sofa in the family room watching television on the large screen. Since the night of the kiss, they'd retreated to their separate rooms each evening, and he hadn't expected to have to face her before going out tonight.

"Nice outfit," she said with a cute whistle, rising to her feet.

He stopped and walked into the room, his gaze

drawn to her pajamas. She was totally covered, wearing a navy silk pair of pants and a long-sleeve top, makeup free, her hair pulled into a messy knot on her head. So why did he find her so damned sexy anyway?

"Hot date?" she asked lightly, but they both knew it was more than a fly-by question.

He managed a shrug. "It's a business thing." And he wasn't going alone.

Arielle Costas was his date. Since the gala fell on the one weekend she was in town, he'd invited her before Maxie had moved in and his life had turned upside down.

"Umm…" He searched for a way to explain.

"Never mind." She waved a hand awkwardly in front of her. "I shouldn't have said anything. It's none of my business."

But he wanted to elaborate. And he needed to, because tonight's event included a red-carpet walk-in and would be covered on the local news and tech blogs, and Maxie might see. And get the wrong idea.

"I'm taking Arielle," he said, forcing the words out.

She blinked in surprise. "I see."

He doubted she understood. He wouldn't if the situation were reversed. Jealousy would eat at him despite the fact that they had no relationship other than friendship.

Normally he had no problem with his and Arielle's

bi-yearly get-togethers, but knowing Maxie thought he'd been engaged to her made this feel awkward.

And wrong.

"We get together once or twice a year, and this event coincided with her trip to New York."

She nodded. "I get it. You don't owe me an explanation. I'm just going back to watching TV. Have fun." She waved in dismissal.

So he walked out and went to pick up Arielle. She wore a silver gown that clung to her curves. He'd always found the brunette attractive. He'd even contemplated making a move before nixing the idea of mixing business and pleasure, but her obvious beauty did nothing for him now. Not when a sad-eyed blonde waited at home.

He endured the flashing of the cameras and the long speeches that followed. Arielle made small talk during dinner, both with the other couples at their table and with him, but it must have been obvious his mind wasn't in the present.

"Where are you?" she asked. "For the record, I'm asking for the second time. Which makes me wonder if I've gotten boring or you just aren't paying attention?" she asked, always blunt and to the point. Something he admired about her.

"I'm sorry." He picked up her hand. "It really is good to see you, but you're right. I'm not really here."

A knowing smile lifted her lips. "Then where are you? Because I've never seen you so preoccupied. And if you don't want me to be insulted, you'd better tell me everything."

He let out a laugh. "I didn't know you were so nosey."

"That's because you've never given me anything to wonder about before. You were always so focused on business, full of questions and ideas. And we both know how much this event means to you. But you're off in your own head, and I can't help but be intrigued." She leaned in closer. "Who is she?"

"What makes you think it's a woman that has me distracted?"

"Oh, please." She waved a hand through the air. "You have a one-track mind. A female is the only thing that could get your focus off business. Do I need to repeat myself?"

"She's my ex-sister-in-law."

"Ooh, that's intriguing."

"I think I like the business side of you better than the busybody one," he said lightly. He didn't mind the questions, because he needed someone to talk to. A friend who would listen and be gone the next day seemed like the perfect solution.

She grinned and took a sip of champagne. "I want details."

She already knew about his brother's death, so he filled her in on the more recent events, Maxie's financial troubles, and how she was now living with him. He even dropped in information about his childhood crush and his brother's need to best him at every turn.

"He even told Maxie we were engaged in order to get her to stop thinking about me," he admitted.

Arielle burst out laughing. "Oh my God. We could never be together. We'd kill each other in the space of one night. You're handsome, but your constant business talk drives me insane."

"Maxie and I never talk business." And he enjoyed his time with her.

"Does it bother you? That you don't have that in common?" Arielle asked.

He shook his head. "It's a nice break from the monotony of my life and how my brain works on a regular basis."

"As they say, opposites attract. So let me ask you something. Why are you here with me and not home with her?"

Lucas grinned, the answer coming easily. "Good question. You ready to get out of here?"

She rolled her eyes. "I find these events as tedious as you do. Let's go."

He was out of his seat in an instant, ready to head

home to Maxie.

MAXIE COULDN'T READ. She couldn't concentrate on TV. And she couldn't sleep. All she could think about was Lucas on a business date with the beautiful Arielle Costas. And if she'd been jealous years before, tonight she was sick to her stomach. Even though she'd pushed him away, she didn't want him with anyone else.

God, what was wrong with her? She had no right to keep Lucas from being friends with another woman. She had even less right to prevent him from dating someone.

She'd already eaten too much of her favorite mint chocolate chip ice cream and rose, walked to the kitchen, and threw out the container.

As she headed back to her room, she pondered her reasons for not wanting to get involved with Lucas. She'd recently recovered from a severe bout of post-partum depression, was living with him because she had no savings, and wanted to stand on her own. Bad timing, she'd thought the other day. But for years, Keith had dictated the timing. He'd lied and schemed to keep them apart.

Lucas was different. He'd apologized for pulling strings to get her a job interview, and he'd promised to respect her need for independence. So what was holding her back? For the first time in her adult life, she was answering only to herself. Why couldn't she indulge in something she'd wanted for what seemed like forever?

She bit down on her lower lip and walked over to the drawer where she'd put her nightclothes and reached into the back, pulling out the black teddy she'd purchased almost right after she'd gotten pregnant. Sex was usually an unsatisfying quickie for her but obviously not for her husband. She hadn't known she was pregnant when she'd bought the lingerie. She'd just wanted things to get better.

She'd purchased the nightie and hoped to put it on after Keith came home. But he'd walked into the house drunk, and she'd smelled perfume on his clothes. Needless to say, the lingerie still had tags on it. That had been the beginning of the end, the pregnancy a surprise but one she'd cherished.

She'd always wanted to be a mother... at least back then. Before she experienced the utter pain and devastation of loss. Now she just wanted to live her life and avoid hurt wherever possible.

She wanted to be happy. She deserved that after all she'd been through, and really, who was her being with Lucas hurting? She held up the sexy teddy and her heart beat harder inside her chest. Did she have the nerve to wear it and approach Lucas? Assuming he came home alone, his date just friendship as he'd claimed. One thing she knew for sure, she couldn't go on torturing herself like this.

She headed for her bathroom, showered with her favorite strawberry-scented wash, shaved, and followed up with creamy lotion to moisturize her skin. She dried her hair, letting it fall around her shoulders.

Then she climbed into bed and waited for Lucas to come home.

LUCAS WAS DISAPPOINTED to find the lights out when he walked into the apartment. He'd been hoping Maxie would still be awake and watching television. Waiting for him? He wouldn't be that presumptuous, but nothing wrong with wishful thinking.

He tossed his keys into the holder on his way to his room, pausing outside Maxie's closed door. He stood, listening to the quiet in the apartment and the sound of his own breath, as he strained to hear any noises inside.

He tipped his head against the door, imagining her asleep in her bed, blonde hair tousled over the sheets, pale skin lit by the moonlight from the window.

Shit. He really had it bad.

Of course, he'd been wanting her his entire life.

He lifted his head and stepped back, about to go to his room, when her door opened, and his breath caught in his throat. She stood before him in a black teddy, her breasts full and plump over the lace trim, the V between them cut deep, revealing her enticing cleavage. His gaze traveled lower, his mouth watering at the sight of the see-through material molding to her waist and full hips.

"You're home early," she said, meeting his gaze.

"Those things bore me."

"The company too?" she asked, obviously referring to Arielle.

He raised one shoulder. "We'd both done enough of the meet-and-greet. I couldn't wait to get home." His voice dropped an octave, his meaning clear. He hoped. He wanted to get back here. To her.

He let his stare roam over her gorgeous body silhouetted in the doorframe. "Where are your long-sleeve pajamas?" he asked.

"They weren't suitable for my needs." She stepped closer, *her* meaning clear.

His heart began to pound harder in his chest. Yes, she was coming on to him, but she was also taking a different stand than she had when she'd backed off a few weeks ago. He needed her to be sure.

Then again, she was greeting him in lace lingerie. Did he really need any more obvious indication than that?

He slid his finger beneath the thin strap holding up the garment and traced the indentation in her flesh. "So this is for me?"

She managed a breathy nod. "I've been waiting for you to get home."

"Why the change of heart?" he asked.

She slid her tongue across her glistening lips. "I want you, Lucas. I always have. I decided it's our time."

He couldn't argue with that logic. Instead he acted. He lifted her into his arms and headed for his bedroom, aware he was one step closer to his ultimate dream.

MAXIE WRAPPED HER arms around Lucas for the walk to his room, her heart soaring, desire racing through her. With every step he took, her barely clad body molded enticingly against his. Her nipples abraded against the lapels of his jacket, and her sex rubbed against his hard erection. Sparks of need rushed over her, making her want *more*.

She threaded her fingers through his hair and inhaled his delicious masculine scent while rubbing her pussy against his cock.

"Slow, or I'm going to explode," he said, just as he

pushed through his door and walked them into the darkened room.

He laid her down on the bed, then reached for the lamp on the nightstand. "I want to see you naked," he said gruffly.

Her cheeks burned with embarrassment but she understood. "I want to see you too."

"Your wish is my command." He unhooked the bow tie, tossing the black strap onto the floor.

His next move was to undo the cuffs. Then he attacked his shirt, one button at a time, until he reached the bottom, shrugging off the shoulders and adding it to the pile of clothes at his feet.

The man worked out hard, because the muscles on his arms and abs were huge, and her fingers itched to touch and squeeze each one. His hands went to his waist and her mouth went dry. And when he lowered his pants, removing his briefs along with them, she lost any moisture in her mouth that remained.

He was huge and erect. His cock jutted out thick and long, and she was overwhelmed with the thought that soon he'd be inside her.

She squirmed, growing slick between her thighs, the bottom of the teddy damp. "My wish has been granted," she murmured. "And exceeded."

"Glad to hear it. Because so has mine." He grinned and joined her on the bed, the mattress dipping with his muscle and weight.

He leaned down and brushed a kiss over her shoulder, and she trembled, her nipples hardening even more. And as his hard erection brushed against her leg, a wave of longing washed over her.

"We need to get you naked too." He reached between her thighs and released the snaps holding her teddy together, revealing her sex for his view.

He sucked in a deep breath and leaned down, pressing a kiss against her pussy. She trembled as his warm breath fanned her slick folds.

"You smell as good as you look," he said, his eyes gleaming with desire.

"Oh my God, Lucas. You really do say what you think," she said, blushing at his frank words.

"No reason not to. Now, this outfit is sexy as fuck, but it's time to get you out of it."

She wriggled and he pulled the material up and over her head, freeing her, leaving her naked.

He groaned, his hot, sexy body coming down on hers. "Now *this* is heaven." He braced himself over her, gliding his cock over her clit.

Sparks of arousal shot through her veins, and she shuddered beneath him. "I didn't know you were a tease," she said, running a hand over his clean-shaven jaw.

"Well, you do now." He reached down and cupped

her breast in his hand, kneading the flesh while brushing his thumb back and forth over her distended nipple.

The sensation shot straight to her sex, and her hips lifted off the bed of their own volition. He moved his hand to the other breast, fondling her flesh. But he wasn't finished. He dipped his head and caught the original nipple between his teeth. He tugged on the tight bud, licked where he'd lightly bitten, then suckled her nipple hard between his lips.

She whimpered with need, slipping her hand between her legs and sliding her finger over her clit, seeking relief.

A hard slap to her thigh followed. She let out a surprised squeak, and she met Lucas' serious stare.

"Do you really think I waited this long so you could get yourself off?" he asked with a cocky, amused grin.

She removed her hand, surprised she now felt the sting on her thigh directly on her clit.

"I guess not. By all means, take over." She waited for him to ease the need growing between her thighs, but instead he continued to play with her breasts, taking his time and arousing her with every lick, lap, and taste.

The weight of his cock grew heavy against her thigh, and she would have reached for him, but his erection was trapped between them, leaving her no choice but to focus on her own desire.

He played with her breasts, teaching her how sensitive she was there. Nobody had taken their time with them before, especially not—She pushed the thought away. She didn't want anyone in this bed except her. And Lucas.

And she wanted Lucas to ease her growing ache. He finally slid a hand down her stomach until he cupped her sex against his hot palm. Red-hot desire flooded her along with a wave of arousal that had her body ready to explode. But the frustrating man was taking his time.

She swore there'd be payback when it was her turn, but in the meantime, he inflamed every one of her senses with his talented tongue, drawing lazy licks down her belly, teasing her across her bikini line and down to her clit. But he never touched her there. He aroused her by playing around, her flesh pulsing with unsated need.

Until finally he slipped one long finger inside her, and she saw stars, her body beginning to peak.

"You're going to come for me," he said before curving his finger in just the right way, rubbing against her inner walls until she began to do just that.

Her body was primed, sensitive, and deprived of intimate contact for too long. She immediately began to shake, her entire being coming apart in a glorious explosion that consumed her. She lost track of time and place, the sensations and warmth shooting through her over and over.

He stayed with her, pumping his finger in and out, until she collapsed against the bed, her body limp and sated. The sound of a crinkling condom wrapper penetrated the fogginess in her brain. At just the thought of him sliding into her, their bodies connecting, she grew wet and ready once more.

He held on to his thick cock and eased the condom over his straining erection with remarkable ease. Watching him ready himself to enter her was incredibly arousing, and she couldn't take her eyes off him, her body pulsing, damp and eager.

"I want you, Maxie. And I want you to feel every inch of me as I take you," he said as he aligned the head of his cock with her opening.

She wasn't used to so much talking during sex, and being with Lucas had her soaring and sublimely happy. From how he looked at her, like he wanted to devour her whole, to how his words rumbled out of him, deep and aroused, she felt wanted and special.

And she wanted him to feel the same way. For whatever this was, however long it lasted, he deserved to know he'd already given her more than she'd ever had before.

"Lucas," she murmured, and he halted before entering her.

"Are you okay, baby?"

"So good. That's what I wanted to tell you."

A slow grin lifted his lips. "Glad to hear it. We're okay then?"

He was asking permission, and her heart melted because she knew he'd do whatever she wanted.

"I want you, Lucas. And everything you make me feel."

He replied with a groan and thrust deep inside her body, joining them together for the first time. He stilled, giving her time to adjust to his size, and soon she felt him pulsing inside her, desire building.

"God, you feel good. So tight and wet around me."

She pulled her knees up, drawing him in deeper, and he began to move, driving into her harder with each thrust, hitting just the right spot. She caught his rhythm, and they moved in sync, a dance of bodies that started slow and quickly grew faster.

Her body tingled, and waves of pleasure washed over her with each successive plunge home until everything inside and out detonated, her orgasm an explosion of bright lights and sensation that filled her, body, heart, and soul.

"Yes, Maxie, baby." He came seconds later, pulsing inside her, causing another ripple of an orgasm to shatter her once more.

It wasn't enough for him to devastate her with the best sex ever, but he had to then get up, walk to the bathroom, clean up, and return with a warm washcloth for her. Next thing she knew, he pulled her into his arms, tucked her head beneath his chin, and fell asleep.

MAXIE WOKE UP disoriented. It took her a few minutes to remember where she was. Not just in Lucas' apartment but in his bed. Alone. She drew a deep breath and calmed her rapidly beating heart.

It was one night, she reassured herself. She could handle it. She'd prepared herself ahead of time, gotten exactly what she wanted. And more, a little voice reminded her. The delicious soreness between her legs agreed.

She grabbed her nightie, pulled on a tee shirt he'd left on the end of the bed, and tiptoed to her own room. She took a shower and dressed, leaving her hair wet and pulled on top of her head. A pair of sweats, a tee shirt, and a casual attitude, and she was ready to walk out of her room.

She followed the smell of breakfast food to the kitchen and found Lucas. He stood by the stove wearing a pair of black track pants, a white untucked tee shirt, and bare feet, cooking French toast, something she remembered his mother making when they were growing up.

"Smells good," she murmured.

He turned and grinned. "I picked up a few tips."

She bit the inside of her cheek. "You didn't need to cook for me."

"How about I wanted to?" He gestured to a chair with the spatula, indicating she should sit down.

She settled into a seat and drank some orange juice he'd poured for them both. The tart taste helped wake her up even more than the shower had.

He served them both a plate with three slices of French toast on each. She poured syrup over hers, and when her stomach rumbled, she realized how hungry she was.

"Guess you worked up an appetite," he said, winking as he shoveled a few pieces into his mouth.

Oh God. "Lucas—"

"Don't want to hear it," he said, wiping his mouth. "We both wanted last night, and I'm not going to listen to any regrets or morning-after recriminations. We didn't do anything wrong."

She opened and closed her mouth again because he was right.

"So what's on tap for today?" he asked.

She tore her gaze from his sexy morning hair and razor stubble. "Nothing. I thought I'd take a walk, get some fresh air." Think about the ramifications of what she'd done—and how he'd made her feel.

He shrugged. "Sounds like fun. I think I'll join you."

She couldn't very well argue… and she didn't want to. Spending the day with him sounded like a perfect afternoon. So what if that meant she could not overthink things. That was probably his intention anyway. Keep her too busy to dredge up issues and problems.

They'd rear their ugly heads soon enough.

LUCAS KNEW IF he gave Maxie time alone, she'd talk herself into believing last night hadn't meant anything, when in reality, it had been everything. He understood her fears and the reasons behind them. She'd been involved with an asshole who wanted to control her, and she was stuck living with another man when she'd rather be asserting her independence in all possible ways.

Lucas had every intention of giving her the freedom she needed to be her own person. He just wasn't giving up on *them* while she explored her new life, and he intended to make her understand the two things weren't mutually exclusive.

Instead of heading to Central Park, which could be

crowded on such a beautiful fall day, they walked down the street, past his apartment, and kept going. A light wind blew around them, and he instinctively wrapped an arm around her to keep her warm. She stiffened in surprise, then eased her body into his as they strode in companionable silence.

They stopped at a vending cart for a hot pretzel and a bottle of water, which they shared.

"So how are you enjoying work?" he asked.

She brushed a long strand of hair from her face. "I love it! It's so different from my last job, but I don't miss dealing with people who I'm not sure whether they're guilty or innocent. I never thought I'd like plain old civil litigation, but it's been interesting. And I really like the lawyers and the staff too."

He glanced her way. Her eyes sparkled with happiness.

"That's great. I'm glad it was a good fit." He paused, wondering if now was the time to share something that was important to him and decided yes. There might not be a better way for her to get to know who he really was. "Speaking of good fits, I want to take you somewhere. Show you something. Are you game?"

She met his gaze, then shrugged. "Sure. Why not?"

He hailed a taxi, and after they climbed in, he gave the driver an address uptown. Not a typical area of the city where you'd visit on a Sunday morning.

"I'm confused," she said as the driver sped toward their destination.

"After Blink took off and we started monetizing it for profit, I wanted to do something more with the money than spend it on myself or put it in the bank." He paused. "Do you remember Eric Kutcher? From middle and high school?"

She nodded. "Did you two stay close?"

He glanced out the car window and saw they still had time for him to explain before they reached their stop.

He didn't answer directly. Not yet. "Kutch went to a small college in California. A technology school his parents thought would be a good fit. And get him away from the bad high school memories."

Kutch had suffered from severe acne and he was overweight. Lucas might have had his brother and occasionally his asshole friends to deal with, but Kutch's bullies took the concept to a whole new level.

"Did you lose touch because of the distance?" she asked.

"You didn't hear?"

"Hear what?" Maxie asked as the cab pulled up to the address Lucas had given.

"Hang on." Lucas paid the driver and asked him to wait. They wouldn't be long here, and even if they were, he wanted to be sure they had a ride back home when they were ready.

He climbed out of the car and helped Maxie out next. "This is it," he said, pointing to a red-brick building.

"Where are we?"

Lucas gestured to a small sign on the side that read, Kutcher Recreation Hall.

Her eyes opened wide. "It's named after him. What happened?"

"If you aren't lucky, reputations follow you, courtesy of social media. Kutch didn't have an easy time of it in college either. He committed suicide freshman year."

"Oh my God." Her hand flew to her mouth, her shock obvious. "I had no idea. My life became so insular I didn't follow high school people on those sites. That's awful. He must have suffered terribly to do that. And his poor parents," she murmured, her eyes filling with tears.

He nodded, recalling the phone call he'd gotten from Kutch's mom. "His parents thought I'd want to know. They called a select few people. Kutch didn't have many friends," Lucas said in a low voice. "I felt like I failed him, losing touch like that. My life took such a different turn. I got lucky. He…" His voice cracked, and he trailed off, unable to express his feelings.

Maxie turned and stepped closer, wrapping her arms around him. "I'm sorry."

"Yeah. Me too." He cleared his throat. "Anyway, this place is a community center and a technology haven. I picked an area that didn't have the money for computers on their own. I figured kids who didn't play sports or have something to do after school could come here. Hang out." He shrugged, almost embarrassed now that he was explaining his motives.

"That's so generous. And such a smart thing for you to do." Her expression was soft and full of understanding.

"I didn't tell you to make me look good. I wanted you to know I didn't forget where I came from. And remind you, while you're wrestling with what happened between us, that I'm nothing like Keith."

She tipped her head back, meeting his gaze with her big brown eyes. "I know. I never should have said you were. I was just upset."

She bit down on her lower lip, a move that had an immediate effect on his groin. But this wasn't the time or the place for him to act on those feelings.

"Lucas, last night was incredible. And I don't regret it. I never could."

"But?" he asked because the follow-up seemed obvious.

"But I can't be in a relationship right now. Not when I'm finding my footing for the first time."

He grasped her hands. "And I respect that. I understand and I plan to give you all the time you need."

"*But*?" she asked this time, with a half-smile on her lips.

"But I'm going to be right here. By your side. I'm not going to let our time pass us by. No way. No how." With that pronouncement, and without waiting for her to respond, he whistled for the cab idling on the street corner, waiting for them.

He'd wanted to have the last word.

Chapter Six

ONCE AGAIN, LUCAS proved himself true to his word. He became a definite presence in Maxie's life. Not that he hadn't been before, but now he stepped up his game. Living together took on a different meaning now that they'd had sex.

Breakfast in the morning was more intimate than it had been before. The car ride to work, though short, provided her with an up-close-and-personal invasion of his personal space because he drove a Porsche, didn't care that he had to pay for expensive New York City parking, and the small interior was filled with his masculine scent. She climbed out of the car even more aware of him than she'd been before she'd gotten inside.

He picked her up afterwards, always agreeing to whatever time she said she had to work until. On later nights, he offered to go out for dinner, and sometimes she was just too tired to cook.

Over the next few weeks, they frequented his favorite restaurants near his apartment. She learned the owners, maître d's, and waiters knew him by name, and he knew theirs and asked about their wives and children.

For as many times as she and Keith had been out to dinner to restaurants he went to often, she never once recalled Keith being friendly to the staff, let alone truly caring about their personal lives. She learned that Lucas had helped put one man's daughter through culinary school because she was just that talented and he couldn't manage it on his waiter salary.

There were so many facets to Lucas' personality, including his standing Thursday boxing night with Derek and often with Kade. He'd come home sweaty and sexy-looking in a tee shirt with the sleeves cut off and the hem ragged at the bottom, the muscles in his legs and arms tight and hard.

But he didn't pressure her to sleep together at night, and to her complete and utter shock, after maintaining she wasn't ready for a relationship and needed distance, she was disappointed. And horny.

Constantly horny.

Every time she lay in her lonely bed at night, she found herself reliving their time together. Her fingers would slide beneath her panties and glide over her wet sex, as she recalled kissing his firm, masculine lips, his delicious taste, and the feel of his thick erection filling her completely. She'd climax knowing he was next door, and instead of putting the night behind her, her desire for a repeat performance was growing.

Living with him only served to bring them closer. They laughed over silly jokes and folded laundry together. They alternated cooking and cleaning, and the routine felt like they were a couple. She didn't know how much longer she could hold out… and the more time that passed, she wondered why she was trying to.

Maxie took a taxi to the storage unit in order to drop off a box of summer clothes she didn't want to have to keep in her room at Lucas', before meeting a friend for lunch at TGI Friday's restaurant. Angela Carson was a paralegal from her job at her old law firm, a curvy woman with wavy brown hair, blue eyes, and a sparkling personality. Last time Maxie had seen Angela was the day she'd left the building for the last time, but they'd kept in touch by text and phone.

Once they were settled and had ordered lunch, they got down to the business of catching up. "So… how's Matt?" she asked of Angela's longtime boy-friend and now her fiancé.

"We finally set a wedding date," Angela said, ex-citement in her voice. "You'd better mark September nineteenth on your calendar."

"I wouldn't miss it," Maxie promised, happy for her friend.

"So tell me about you." Angela leaned forward, eager to hear all. "I hated how the partners left you high and dry just because your husband was a douchebag," she said, then blushed. "I'm sorry. That was thoughtless." She took a sip of her Diet Coke. "Me and my big mouth."

Maxie shook her head. "It can't be thoughtless when it's true. Besides, you know I agree." She tried not to think about Keith at all, but when she did, her thoughts weren't kind ones. The good memories were buried under the bad, beneath a ton of hurt, debt, and betrayal.

"How are things at the firm?" Maxie asked, changing the subject.

"Well, I do have some gossip." Angela rested her elbows on the dark wood table, excitement flickering in her eyes. "Remember Vincent Bernardi?"

Maxie nodded. "He was Keith's client. Accused of embezzlement and racketeering, but the government was still building a case. In the meantime, he went to jail for assault."

"Right. He beat a guy nearly to death," Angela said with a shudder. "Anger issues."

Maxie had done her share of work on that case

too.

Angela twisted the straw in her drink. "Well, he's out and he came to the firm."

"What?" Maxie sat upright, stunned.

"I was tied up in court that day. All I know is he came by and made a scene. He was furious."

"What did he want?" Maxie asked.

"He demanded access to his case files. He left when poor Katie at reception threatened to call the police," Angela said.

"Wow." Maxie leaned back in her chair. "I'm glad I wasn't there," she murmured. She'd never liked Bernardi, and he'd always had a temper.

"So that's my good gossip. What do you have?" Angela asked.

Maxie laughed. "Not much going on with me."

"You're blushing!"

She blew out a deep breath. "There's a guy," she admitted. She went on to explain her entire crazy situation with Lucas.

"Is it a serious relationship?"

She twisted the paper napkin in her hand. "How can I possibly be serious about someone when I'm just getting my independence back? My life back together?"

Angela waved a hand, dismissing her concerns. "You're the strongest woman I know. Living with that bastard and surviving? Come on. You don't give yourself enough credit. Surely you can do both."

Maxie blinked, the thought now stuck in her head. "Can I?"

"Do you want to? Or should I ask... Is he hot? Because I have to tell you, Keith wasn't my type." Angela wrinkled her nose in distaste.

"Angela!" Maxie laughed, the sound coming out more like a snort.

But she had a point. Maxie definitely hadn't chosen Keith as a look-alike substitute for the man she couldn't have. Where Lucas was built and solid, Keith had been lean and... well lawyerly looking, if there was such a thing. Maybe when they were younger, they'd looked more alike. Same hair color, similar features. But she'd never fallen for Keith the way she had for either version of Lucas—the young guy or the sexy man.

"Well, if you must know... Lucas is nothing like his brother. Back when we were teenagers, he was more of an adorable geek. Now he's all grown up. He works out, he bulked up, and he's *hot*."

"From the sound of it, I'd say you have it bad for him."

"I do," she said, ignoring the flush in her cheeks at the admission. She already knew how much she desired him, but that was purely physical. The other day, he'd shown her a deeper part of him than she'd seen before, and it had gotten to her. Now she wanted him because she knew she could trust him. That provided a whole different perspective and scared her a little.

"Girl, why can't you just reach out and take what you want? Sleep with the man if he's that hot." Angela waggled her eyebrows.

Maxie laughed. "I did sleep with him and freaked out after."

"Because you're thinking in terms of a relationship. Think more like a man. Sex for the sake of sex. What's wrong with that?"

"This from the woman engaged to her high school sweetheart? The longest long-term relationship I know?" Maxie asked, a bit enviously. While in her miserable marriage to Keith, she'd longed for what Angela had.

Angela smirked. "Do as I say, not as I do. Does…"

"Lucas."

"Lucas. Hmm. Even his name is sexy. Does he want to sleep with you again?"

Maxie thought back to what he'd said the other day. *I'm not going to let our time pass us by. No way. No how.*

"Yes, he does," she told Angela.

"Then what are you waiting for? Take him up on it

and this time don't run afterward," Angela said, as if it were that simple.

And maybe it was.

"Here you go," the waitress said, arriving with their meals with impeccable timing.

"Thank you," Maxie said as the woman put their dishes on the table.

They began to eat, leaving Maxie alone with her thoughts about her hot guy. And what she was going to do about him.

LUCAS HOPED MAXIE appreciated his restraint, because he was wearing out his hand, taking care of himself to thoughts of thrusting into her wet heat. It was getting to be a morning and evening ritual to take the edge off, but strangely he wasn't losing patience. She was worth the wait.

And this morning he was waiting for a whole different reason. She was running late for work.

"I forgot to set my alarm clock," she said, dashing past him, grabbing her purse, and running back to her room.

A few minutes later, she rushed by him again, grabbing a cup of yogurt from the refrigerator. "I'll eat it at my desk," she said, shoving it into her bag along with a plastic spoon.

"Ready." She exhaled hard and started for the door when her cell rang. She muttered a curse as she took the call. "Hello?" she asked, then listened. "This is she." Some more silence and then, "What do you mean my unit was broken into?"

She ran a hand through her wavy hair and groaned. "Yes, I understand. But I can't get over until lunchtime." She paused. "Yes. Yes. Thanks for calling." She disconnected and met his gaze.

"What was broken into?" he asked.

"My storage unit, of all things. They aren't sure what, if anything, was taken, so they want me to come take a look and file a claim. I'll be lucky if I can figure out if anything is gone."

"I'll go with you," he said and caught her pointed look. "If you want me to," he reluctantly added. Because he was trying to let her handle things on her own.

"Thanks but it's not a big deal. I'll go, take a look around, and see if I can identify anything that's been taken. No big deal."

"If that's what you want." It wasn't what *he* preferred to do. He was learning that it wasn't in his nature to take a step back.

But if he wanted to prove to her he was different from his brother and worthy of her trust, he had to let her handle things on her own.

★ ★ ★

MAXIE'S MORNING WAS rushed from the minute she'd woken up late courtesy of a night debating how to approach Lucas this time. She didn't want to appear wishy-washy, but that's exactly what she'd done. Come on to him, pull back out of fear. She knew she had to make the first move again. And this time be ready to stick out the consequences.

She'd tossed and turned again last night, unsure of whether or not to take that next step. And then this morning, he'd backed off and let her handle her problems with the burglary at the storage unit on her own. That's when she'd asked herself, what more did she need him to prove to her? He clearly understood the parameters she'd set up for them. He understood her. She'd just have to make certain they were on the same page.

Unfortunately, she had no time to talk to him about it today. She was slammed at the office with filings and documents that the attorneys needed prepared, and she worked straight through to a late lunch without a break.

Instead of eating, she took a cab to the storage unit and did a walk-through with one of their employees, but other than things knocked over and broken, she didn't see anything noticeably missing. She filled out a claim form to the best of her ability in the rushed time she had and headed back to work.

It wasn't until around four p.m. when she finally had a chance to catch her breath, grab a quick bite, and think. And when she did, she knew what she had to do.

LUCAS AND HIS partners had a late-afternoon meeting with one of the tech guys. They'd gathered in Lucas' office, and the man was droning on for way too long about a new idea for an algorithm that had potential. Lucas already understood the point. He didn't need to sit here any longer.

He yawned and shot Kade an annoyed look. The other man nodded. He glanced at Derek, who did the same.

"Wrap it up, Mark. We'll discuss your suggestions and figure out where to go from here," Lucas said.

The other man, one of their young, brilliant talents, summed up his pitch and left the room.

"Thank God," Lucas muttered. He wanted nothing more than to head home.

"I couldn't agree with you more. Lexie's home waiting." Kade grinned.

"I really don't need to know you're going to get laid," Derek muttered.

Lucas coughed.

Kade shot Derek a nasty look. "Hey, that's Lexie you're talking about."

Derek held up one hand in apology. "Right. I got it."

"No, you don't. But someday I figure you will." Kade rose to his feet, and both he and Derek made their way out, shutting the door behind them.

Lucas began to pack up his laptop along with some work to take home when his desk phone rang. He picked it up quickly. "Yes, Tessa?"

"You have a visitor," she said.

"Whoever it is, I'm done for the day. And you can get going too," he told her.

Lucas might not have a woman waiting for him the way Kade did, but he got to see Maxie at the end of the day, and that was enough to lure Lucas away from work.

"Okay, boss. I'm sorry, Ms. Sullivan, Mr. Monroe isn't seeing anyone today," Lucas heard Tessa say before she disconnected their call.

Maxie was here?

He jumped up from his seat and nearly vaulted across his desk in an effort to make sure she didn't leave before he could get there.

He swung open the door, catching sight of her standing beside Tessa. Dressed in the same work clothes from this morning, she wore a simple black skirt that hit above the knee, heels, and a cream-colored blouse that showed off her luscious curves. Her hair, clipped off her face, fell over her shoulders in sexy waves.

His breath hitched just looking at her. "I'll see her," he called out to Tessa, who stared at him as if he'd lost his mind.

He'd probably burst through the door like a lunatic, and this woman was to blame.

"Maxie, come on in." He gestured for her to join him, and she walked around Tessa's desk and brushed past him as she entered.

He shut the door behind them and, because he didn't want to be disturbed, locked it with a press of a button.

He wondered what she was doing here. He'd texted her after lunch, asking about the storage unit, and she'd said not to worry, all was fine. She hadn't answered his reply, so he figured she was busy and he'd see her when he picked her up from work.

He walked to his desk, turned, and leaned against the aluminum, meeting her gaze. "Hey," he said lightly.

She stood a few steps away from him. "Hi." Her lips lifted in a smile.

He folded his arms across his chest. "So, this is a surprise."

She inclined her head and nodded. "If you're busy,

I can see you at home later."

"I'm never too busy for you. What's up?"

She swallowed hard. "I had a revelation." Her cheeks flushed at the admission, piquing his curiosity.

She placed her bag on the chair Kade had been sitting in earlier and stepped closer.

"What kind of revelation?" he asked, knowing it could be good or bad.

She clasped her hands tightly in front of her, obviously gathering her courage. "Would you agree that we've been... on hold?" she asked. "Since that night when we were together?"

His breath left him in a sharp rush. He hadn't expected her to go *there*. All he'd been able to think about was them together, his cock deep inside her, and repeating that night. Hell yes, they'd been on hold. And his body wasn't happy with being deprived of what it wanted, especially when she was in the room next door.

"I agree. Although I made it clear that's not what I want," he reminded her.

She sucked her bottom lip between her teeth, and his cock jerked in his pants.

"Well, I realized I don't want us to be apart anymore either." She stepped closer, her fruity scent an arousing addition to his inhale.

He waited for her to continue, because as far as he

was concerned, this conversation could go anywhere.

"I backed off because I needed to know I could stand on my own. But I realize now I can do both. Be independent and be with you." She glanced up at him through thick lashes. "And you proved you understand what I need. I mean, today, you let me handle the storage unit without insisting you needed to come along. You respect me."

"I do."

She lifted a finger and let it trail down his chest, but he didn't respond to the bait. Instead he waited, because his gut told him there was more to this turnaround, and he needed to hear it all.

"So I know we can … have sex and I won't lose myself in any way."

And there it was.

And though her eyes shone bright in her face as she admitted the reason she'd come to see him, her words didn't bring him the relief he'd have thought.

And he knew why.

"Sex," he said, repeating her word choice. "You're here because you want to fuck again?"

He was deliberately cold and crude, and she blinked at his harsh tone, her hand dropping from where she'd been touching his shirt. "Lucas, I didn't mean—"

"Yes, you did. Or you would have said it differently. So let's be clear. You aren't here because you want a relationship." Which he did.

With Maxie it was all or nothing, at least for him. Clearly she had other ideas.

"I thought you understood. I'm barely out of my marriage, and I'm dependent on you for where I live. So no, I'm not ready for a relationship. But I don't see why that means I have to deny us what we both want."

On the surface, he understood her point. He, too, wanted her to be the self-respecting woman he knew she could be. And would be soon. But she was demeaning what he felt for her... what they could be together. And yet again, he understood.

Still, he ought to be offended that she was turning to him for sex... but he wasn't. The fact was, Maxie was feeding herself a line of BS. They already were in a relationship. If you defined one by confiding in each other, sharing meals, sharing living space—and once they crossed this next line, they would be sharing a bed. He'd see to it. To him, that was a relationship.

If she wanted to delude herself into thinking they were just having sex, he would let her go on thinking that—hence his use of cold words—until she was ready for more.

There was just one more box he needed to check off in the non-relationship/relationship department, at least in his own mind.

"This sexual relationship has to be exclusive. That's nonnegotiable."

She nodded. "Of course."

He held back a grin. She didn't know what to make of his responses, and that was good. She was off-balance. Unable to think too clearly. She'd come here wanting to take that next step, but their conversation hadn't left her in seductress mode.

Fine with him. He had no problem taking over.

Chapter Seven

L UCAS' WOLFISH EXPRESSION was enough to cause a near-orgasm, his grin and the yearning in his gaze were that potent. Everything about the man was sexy, from his smile to the tattooed, muscled forearm peeking out from his tee shirt to how good he smelled.

She wanted nothing more than to be in his arms, but her head spun from their conversation about sex. She'd intended to approach him and hopefully seduce him again. She hadn't expected such a frank talk, nor had she anticipated somehow hurting his feelings when she expressed her desires.

"Maxie?" he asked.

She blinked at the sound of his voice. And yeah, that, too, was hot. "Yes?"

"Quit worrying so much," he ordered. "And come here."

"I'm that obvious, hmm?"

He nodded, that grin widening. "But it's cute."

She blushed at the description. "I'm not sure that's the word I was aiming for."

He crooked a finger at her. "Get over here and let's seal our deal."

Now that she could do. "With pleasure."

She stepped closer, not realizing her arms were folded over her chest until he grasped her elbows and pulled her against him, his lips coming down hard on hers.

She gasped and wound her arms around his neck, her legs wrapping around his waist. With a groan, he spun her around and backed her against the desk, his groin hard and thick against her sex. She wriggled against him, attempting to get even closer, letting the waves of desire wash over her as his cock hit just the right spot.

"Lucas," she murmured, the sensations rolling through her.

"I've got you," he said, setting her down on top of the cool desktop. He stepped between her thighs. Meeting her gaze, he cupped her face in his hand. "You want sex?" he asked.

She couldn't let him go on thinking that's all there was between them, but she couldn't get involved any deeper. "I want *you*."

"I want you too, beautiful." He stood her up and

undid her skirt, sliding it to the floor.

"There are people in the office," she squeaked.

"And I locked the door from the inside."

Privacy was all she needed. When he hooked a hand in her panties and drew them down her legs, she shifted her hips to help him, then kicked the skirt and panties to the side, struggling as they caught in the heel of her shoe.

He stepped back and looked her over, his dark, heated gaze devouring her from head to toe. "So damned sexy," he muttered.

Beneath his heady gaze, she felt sexy. And wanted.

Without warning, he spun her around. "Hands on the desk."

At his gruff tone, she grew wetter between her thighs. She did as he asked, bracing her hands against the cool surface.

From behind her, she heard the sounds of him undoing his zipper. She looked over her shoulder as he dropped his pants and boxer briefs to the floor, kicking them off.

Then he was behind her, hands on her upper back, leaning her over the desktop. Her breasts pressed against the aluminum, a surprisingly arousing sensation of cool metal against her silk-covered nipples.

He cupped one ass cheek in his big hand and squeezed so hard she might have his fingerprints there the next day. But not only did his touch feel good, tomorrow she'd be reminded of this moment and of Lucas. She purred at the thought.

"I dreamed about this," he said as he slid one hand between her thighs and captured her slickness in his fingertips, spreading the moisture over her sex. "You, bent over my desk, me taking you from behind."

The next sound she heard was the crinkling of a condom package. He stepped back and soon returned, nudging the head of his cock inside her. She gasped at the initial breach, sighed at the pulsing sensation of him gliding home, hitting deeper than he had the last time.

"Oh God." She cried out, and he cupped his hand over her mouth.

"Do you want the whole office banging down the door to see what's going on?"

She shook her head hard. *I'll be quiet*, she thought, but couldn't say the words out loud. Instead she licked at his hand, nipping at his salty flesh.

He groaned and pulled out. She felt the loss for a split second too long before he tunneled back into her again. Her fingers clawed at the desk as he began to take her at a steady pace. One that, with each thrust, brought her body higher, had her soaring beyond anything she'd experienced in her life.

He pulled at her hair, tipping her head back so he

could nuzzle at her neck with every push into her. "I'm close," he said, the words coming out like a groan in her ear. "And I'm not coming alone."

He reached around and slid one finger over her clit. Thunder roared and light flashed behind her eyes as her climax hit. He slammed into her once, twice more, coming with a roar and her name echoing around her.

She breathed heavily, her cheek against the desk as he collapsed against her, his big body pinning her down, his breath rumbling roughly against her.

Finally, he stood up. Pulled out. And she felt the loss. Between her thighs, she felt a sweet ache. Though she heard the rustling sound of his pants behind her, she couldn't move.

Not until he lifted her up, brushing her hair out of her face. "You okay?" he asked, his expression concerned.

"Never better," she murmured, but she was suddenly aware of the stickiness on her legs and being half-naked in his office.

She started for her clothes, but he beat her to it, scooping her skirt and panties off the floor. "Here." He knelt down, holding them for her to step into.

Her skirt followed, and she tucked herself in, fixing herself though she knew it was going to be perfectly obvious what they'd been doing in here.

Which brought a flush to her face. "Well, that was…"

"Great sex?" he asked, winking at her.

It was. But they both knew it had also been so much more.

Lucas called ahead and ordered dinner for them to pick up on their way home. When they arrived at the apartment, she announced her intention to shower before dinner, and he said he'd do the same. There was no awkward discussion, and she was grateful for the escape and the chance to catch her breath. Still, she didn't overthink things, instead rushed to get ready for dinner. They ate pizza and a salad and cleaned up together. Again, casual, relaxed, and easy.

He was obviously going to respect her boundaries, and she breathed out a sigh of relief. She refused to wonder why a part of her was disappointed he wasn't pushing for more.

She turned in for the night, changed into her favorite comfy tee shirt, brushed her teeth, and settled in to read. Twenty minutes later, a knock sounded on her door.

Knowing it was Lucas, her stomach flipped in excitement, and her body softened in anticipation. Darn it. She couldn't even think about him being on the other side of the wall without wanting him.

She put her reader down, slid out of bed, and

opened the door.

He stood in a pair of gray sweats hanging low on his hips and nothing more. She came face-to-face with the sexy razor stubble on his beard and the ink down his arm and across his rib cage.

God, he was hot.

"Hi," she said, her voice hoarse.

"Hi." His gaze slid down her body, his stare focused on the words on her shirt: *Let's kill all the lawyers.* "Shakespeare. Cute."

She blushed. "I wasn't expecting company."

His grin turned to a frown. "You weren't?"

"Umm, no."

"So you thought after committing to wanting to… have sex, you were going to sleep alone."

She blinked in surprise. "Well, I didn't think we'd be sleeping together."

He let out a long-suffering sigh. "Well, if I'm going to be in an exclusive sexual relationship, I definitely want to enjoy the perks of that."

She frowned at his stark reference to how he'd decided to define their situation. At least he hadn't called them fuck buddies, she thought irritably, knowing she deserved it but not liking the feeling anyway.

"So? Your room or mine?" he asked too cheerfully. "Yours is nice, but I should mention that I have a king-size bed."

She leaned on the doorframe. "You're welcome to sleep in your large bed by yourself."

"Really?" he asked, not even looking wounded. "Because I think having you in it would be so much more fun. Your bed or mine? Decide. One... two... three."

When she didn't immediately respond, he bent and picked her up, hefting her over his shoulder, holding her still with one hand on her barely covered backside. "Mine it is," he said, and headed for his room.

"Lucas! Put me down!" She clung to the top of his sweat pants, well aware her knuckles were brushing his bare ass.

"Okay." He flipped her over, her back hitting the mattress, and she shut her eyes to get her bearings.

"You're insane!"

"I'm just clarifying how things are going to be."

She narrowed her gaze. "Didn't I say I wanted to be in charge of my own life?"

He grinned. The one that showed all those white teeth and was impossible to resist. "You are most definitely in charge of your own life. It's just that I'm in charge in the bedroom. Did I forget to mention that during our negotiation?"

"Negotiation? You're making me crazy," she muttered.

He dove onto the bed and rolled on top of her.

"That's the point. Can't you just shut down the worry and enjoy?" He kissed the tip of her nose. One eyelid. Then the other.

"Can you do that for me?"

"Mmm. You make it sound so easy."

"That's because it is." He rolled to the side and she did the same. "Go with the flow."

"It's been years since I've had that luxury."

"Then let me give that to you." He rubbed his cheek against hers. "Okay? Can you do that?"

"Yeah, I can." Because she wanted to be with him, and for now that's what mattered.

He yawned and she smiled. "Tired?"

"You have no idea." He hooked their legs together and curled his big body around hers. "You wore me out earlier today." He wrapped an arm around her, pulled her tighter, and began to breathe easily in and out.

Sleep didn't come as quickly for Maxie. She wasn't used to sleeping with someone else. Not even when she'd been married. Keith had been a take what he wanted, roll over, and go to sleep kind of guy. At first it had hurt her feelings but as things degenerated, she'd been grateful for the distance.

Lucas, it seemed, had no intention of allowing her space.

A WEEK LATER, the assistants, Tessa, Becky, and Kade's wife, Lexie, had called a morning meeting, asking the three bosses to attend. They'd plied the men with coffee before giving their pitch.

"I'm not doing a Halloween party here," Derek said with a shake of his head.

"Why not?" Becky, Derek's assistant, asked. "It'll be good for morale. You know the tech guys downstairs would love to come dressed up."

Tessa glanced at Lucas. "And you'd be giving them a chance to bring a significant other to meet their coworkers."

"Oh, now we're paying for significant others?" Kade asked, his gaze on his wife.

Lexie shot him a pleading glance. "Please? It'll be so much fun." She turned to face Lucas. "I called Maxie this morning and made lunch plans. I thought it would be nice to get to know her better. And I might have mentioned something about a fun Halloween party here," she said in a rush, then turned her gaze back to Kade.

"You know you need to rein her in," Lucas said.

Kade burst out laughing. "Let's have this conversation in another month or so. Let's see how much reining in *you're* doing then."

"Dammit, we're going to have to do this, aren't we?" Derek muttered, glaring at his assistant, who never quite took him seriously.

"Did Maxie seem interested in the party?" Lucas asked.

Lexie grinned. "She did. She might have mentioned something about wanting to be Catwoman. And that would solve your costume problem. You could go as Batman." She sounded pleased with herself.

Lucas' mind immediately went to a vision of Maxie in a leotard outlining her curvy body, a cape, tights on her long, sexy legs, and cat ears on her head. And if she could find an outfit with snaps between her legs like that hot-as-fuck lingerie she'd worn for him their first night, this party was sounding like a better idea by the minute.

"I'm almost afraid to ask what costume that leaves for us," Kade said, pulling Lucas' focus back to the discussion at hand.

"It's a go!" Lexie clapped her hands, and Tessa raised her fingers in a victory sign.

"I can't wait! Let's go pick a date." Lexie raised herself up on her heels and pressed a kiss to Kade's cheek. "Thank you!"

She turned to Lucas and hugged him briefly before doing the same to Derek, who was muttering to himself about women. And men being whipped.

He was not wrong.

A few hours later, Tessa knocked on his door and entered without waiting to be asked. "Lucas, you need to get out here quick. Kade's got a guy up against the wall, and I'm afraid he's going to kill him."

Lucas shot out of his chair and rushed for the main area, knowing there was only one man who'd get Kade that worked up. He immediately saw the problem. Kade had Julian Dane pinned against the wall near the elevator.

Their one-time friend, former partner of sorts, and the man who'd blackmailed Kade and tried to get shares of Blink or derail their IPO, had his hands in the air. He obviously wasn't looking for a fight, but Kade wasn't listening.

"Kade." Lucas stepped up to them, bracing a hand on his friend's shoulder, hoping to distract him.

"I just want to talk," Julian said.

"Well, I have nothing to say to you."

Lucas understood why. Julian had dated Lexie's sister, pretending to be in love with her, all the while using her to get what he wanted. Unfortunately, Lexie's sister, Kendall, had bipolar disorder and was going through a rough patch at the time. Julian's behavior hadn't helped Kendall's mental state and had nearly broken up Kade and Lexie. So no, Lucas didn't think Kade would take seeing Julian well. At all.

"Then let him go," Lucas suggested.

They didn't need Julian deliberately provoking Kade into hitting him so he could file a lawsuit or, worse, have Kade arrested for assault.

Kade dropped him and, still breathing hard, stepped back, glaring at the other man in disgust. "Get the fuck out."

"I'm just worried about Kendall," Julian said.

Kade let out a bark of disbelief. "The time to worry about her was before you fucked with her head. Now leave before I call the cops and have you arrested for trespassing."

"I'd go if I were you," Lucas said to Julian, punching the elevator button to emphasize his point.

"Fine. I suppose it's too much to tell her I came by?"

Kade started toward him again, and Lucas grabbed him by the arm, pulling him back.

The doors opened and thankfully Julian stepped inside. He glanced at Lucas, and he could swear he saw a hint of regret in Julian's gaze.

Lucas waited until Julian was safely gone before turning to Kade. Around them, the office staff had gathered, to watch and to gossip.

"Come on. Let's go into your office and talk." He slapped Kade on the shoulder and led the way into his friend's office.

Unlike Lucas' messy desk, Kade's setup was stark

and clean, courtesy of his anxiety and OCD tendencies. Kade had himself under control, but a confrontation like this wouldn't be good for him.

"Want me to call Lexie?" Lucas offered.

"No. I don't want her to know about this. She'll get worked up and worried that Julian will get in touch with her sister. Which he'll do over my dead body," Kade muttered.

Kade ran his fingers back and forth over the glass of his Patek Phillipe watch. It wasn't just a symbol of success; it meant something to Kade. Julian had known it and targeted him accordingly, going so far as to get Kendall to steal the watch.

Lucas frowned at the reminder. "Can I get you something to relax you?" He didn't know whether or not to offer Kade a drink.

"No." Kade reached into his pocket and shook out a pill.

Lucas didn't say a word. He just waited for his friend to take it with the bottle of water on his desk. "Kendall's doing better, right?" he asked of Lexie's sister.

"Much. After she checked herself into the treatment center, she really dedicated herself to life changes and improvement. That's why I don't want Julian anywhere near her."

"We can put security on her."

Kade shook his head. "She deserves to live a normal life. But I'm warning you—"

"He'll stay clear. I'll talk to him myself," Lucas promised.

Kade had been about to lift the bottle of water to his mouth and stopped. "You'd deal with that asshole?"

"For you, man? You know I would."

"Thank you," Kade said.

The three men became friends in college, back in their first-year fraternity days, before Lucas had dropped out due to sheer boredom.

But they'd already started working on Blink, and back then, Julian had been a part of things. Before drugs had become more important to him than anything else. As far as Lucas knew, Julian had been clean for a while. He certainly looked clear and stable today.

Lucas nodded. "Go home to Lexie." She was the only person who could completely calm Kade down. From the day they'd met, there'd been an innate bond and understanding, though it'd taken them awhile to get past their initial mistrust.

"I'll do that." Kade ran a hand over his short hair before packing up his things for the day.

"I'll head out with you. Just let me grab my things."

Before he could walk out, Kade asked, "How's it going living with Maxie?"

Lucas was glad his friend was distracted by something other than Julian. "I wouldn't say I have her wrapped around my finger. But … it's going." And they were sleeping together every night, and she wasn't complaining. Far from it. He hoped he had the woman in a sex-induced coma.

But that didn't change her hesitancy about *them* and relationships in general.

"I remember those uncertain days," Kade said. "They were a pain in the ass."

"You can say that again," Lucas muttered. But regardless, he was eager to get home to Maxie.

MAXIE LEFT WORK early, courtesy of the head lawyer on the case she was working on. They'd had a few late days in a row, and he wanted to give them a breather. A far cry from the work, work, work mentality she'd had at her old firm, and it was refreshing.

She was surprised when she heard the key in the lock, and Lucas, too, came home early. He walked into the room looking tired and stressed.

"What's wrong?" She rose from her seat, concerned about him.

He ran a hand along the back of his neck. "Just a

stressful day."

"Want to talk about it?" she asked, reaching out a hand. He took it and she led him to the couch. They both sat down. "What's going on?"

"Early this morning, my biggest problem was a Halloween party the office staff wants to have."

"I heard," she said, smiling. She was looking forward to meeting Lexie for lunch one day soon.

"But this afternoon we had an incident at the office. You know about Julian Dane?"

She nodded. "Lexie told me and you filled me in."

"Well, he decided it was a good idea to pay Kade a visit."

"What? Why?"

He leaned forward, shoulders hunched. "I wish to God I knew. He claimed he was worried about Kade's sister-in-law, Kendall."

"The same woman he used and hurt?"

Lucas nodded. "Kade lost it. I had to pull him off the guy. But—"

She leaned in closer. "But what?"

"Damned if there wasn't something in his eyes. I almost believe he was sincere. Not that I'd admit as much to Kade. And I promised I'd have a talk with Julian. Assess his motives and warn him to stay away from Kendall." Lucas shrugged. "Like I said, stressful day."

"I'm sorry." She pushed herself to the edge of the sofa. "Here. Turn around."

She nudged him so he pivoted away from her, and she began to massage his tense shoulders, digging her fingertips into the muscles and tendons there. She bit down on her lower lip, trying her best to focus on his need and not the desire created by being so close to him. Or the delicious scent of his masculine cologne.

He hung his head forward and groaned. "That feels so damned good." The words came out a low rumble.

Unable to resist, she leaned in, pressed her breasts against his back, wrapped her arms around his neck, and kissed the back of his neck. His entire body trembled at her light touch, but she wasn't finished. Although she'd approached him each time, he'd been in charge. She wanted her turn to make him feel good.

"I know another way to relax you," she whispered huskily in his ear.

"Show me," he said in a gruff voice.

She eased herself around him and slid down between his legs. She undid the button on his pants, then slowly and carefully pulled his zipper over the evidence of his desire.

"Lift up."

He did as she asked, and together they maneuvered his pants, along with his boxer briefs, down to his ankles. She stared down at his straining erection, a drop of precum glistening on top, and need rushed through her at the sight.

She looked up and found his eyes darkened with hunger. No man had ever looked at her with such stark lust before, and it was a heady feeling.

She reached out and cupped his erection in her hand, gliding up and down the thick shaft.

"Harder."

Her gaze flew to his, but she tightened her grip and began to move her hand up and down, his cock hot and heavy in her hands. He groaned, clenching his fists at his sides, eyes closed, head thrown back, the cords in his neck visible and straining.

She liked having this effect on him, and she was arousing herself as well, but she knew she could do more. She removed one hand, leaned down, and wrapped her mouth around his shaft.

"Oh fuck," he said on a groan.

Smiling, at least in her head, she swirled her tongue over the tip, tasting the saltiness, licked around the head and beneath the sensitive underside. When she sucked hard, he grasped her hair and began to guide her up and down, the sting a welcome sensation, adding to the ache between her thighs.

She continued her ministrations, her sole focus on giving him intense pleasure. He pumped his hips, his cock hitting the back of her throat. She drew a breath through her nose and managed to swallow around him.

"Not like this." He tugged at her hair and she lifted her head.

"Skirt off," he said.

She met his hot gaze and slid the garment down and off, along with her panties. She swung one leg over his lap until his erection aligned with her sex when reality struck. "Condom."

"Shit. Bedroom drawer."

The head of his cock teased her mercilessly, and she moaned.

Knowing there was no way she would risk getting pregnant, she ran for the bedroom and retrieved the packet. She ripped it open and rolled it down his straining shaft before resuming her position, straddling him, his cock at her opening, and sliding down.

They groaned in unison, his gaze meeting hers, the connection intimate as he entered her, thick and pulsing, filling her completely.

"Ride me, beautiful."

At his words, her heart caught in her throat, but she did as he said, lifting herself up and falling back down on his erection. As she rose, his cock slid out, hitting every sensitive spot inside her, then struck again on the way back down. She rocked forward, her clit hitting his pubic bone, and sensation darted through her veins, feeling oh so good.

Instead of lifting herself up and down, she grabbed his shoulders and rolled back and forth, waves of arousal building inside her. Faster. Higher. He met her movement, rocking his hips in time to hers.

He slid his hand between them and rubbed her clit. Stars flickered behind her eyes.

"Look at me," he said in that commanding voice he only used during sex, his hand, as usual, wrapped in her hair.

She immediately complied, their gazes locked intimately on one another. He pressed hard on her clit, and she flew apart, ripples vibrating through her as she cried out his name. He continued his upward thrusts, until he, too, came with a roar, his big body shaking beneath hers.

His muscles finally went lax, and he dropped forward, his forehead touching hers, his breath rough. "You can relax me any time," he said on a laugh.

She chuckled, then realized she was the one who'd have to break contact this time. "Umm…" She gingerly rose and climbed off him, knelt down, grabbed her underwear and skirt, and headed for the bathroom.

Just as she turned on the shower, he grasped her hips, pulling her naked buttocks into him. She jumped in surprise, then relaxed against him. "Don't tell me. You're joining me."

"And she reads minds as well as gives one hell of a blow job." He spun her around and winked, then pulled her into a long kiss.

His cock immediately began to thicken again… and the shower took an extra-long time.

Chapter Eight

LUCAS WAS ALONE at the gym. Kade had bailed on their weekly boxing because Lexie wasn't feeling well, and Derek needed to work late with one of the programmers. Lucas had decided to head over anyway. Someone there would spar with him, and then he'd head home.

When he arrived, a lot of the guys were already paired up. Lucas decided to use a bag instead. He pulled on a pair of gloves, and after fifteen minutes, he'd worked up a good sweat.

For the first time in a long time, he didn't have angry aggression to work out, and it felt good to exercise for enjoyment alone. He'd paused to catch his breath when a guy Lucas had never seen before walked up to him.

"Hey."

"Hi." Lucas yanked off a glove. "Are you new

here?"

"I'm scoping out the place." He was a big man, more from food than muscles, and he didn't look like he'd used a gym much in his life. "Want me to hold the bag?" He gestured to the bigger one he normally worked out with when Derek or Kade was around.

Lucas shrugged. "Why not." He held out his hand, and the other man helped pull the glove on. "I'm Lucas Monroe."

"Vinny Bernard. Good to meet you."

As Lucas began his routine, Vinny began to talk. "You come here often?"

Lucas grunted. There wasn't much he could say while bashing a heavy bag.

"So I'm new to the area. Any good restaurants nearby?"

Lucas treated him to another grunt, then hit the bag harder before pausing to catch his breath. "A few. I'll tell you later."

"This gym is really no frills. You like it though?"

Lucas had had enough of this. "I think I'm going to hit the treadmill for a while." Maybe he'd lose his new friend.

But Vinny followed him and hopped on the one next to his.

Lucas hit the buttons and started to run, focused on the TV screen on the panel in front of him. He watched the stock market closing numbers run by.

"I like to work out with my brother, but he's been too busy lately. You got a brother?" Vinny asked.

Lucas groaned. "I have friends I work out with." He wasn't going to get into personal shit with a talkative stranger.

"My brother's older," Vinny went on, oblivious to Lucas' irritation with this chatting and prying. "He's a real pain in the ass in some ways. Thinks he's king shit because he's a big deal on Wall Street. But he's my brother, you know? I'd do anything for him."

Lucas already regretted getting involved with this guy. He grabbed a towel and shut down the treadmill and wiped his face, which was dripping with sweat.

"I have to get home," he said, not bothering with pleasantries. He didn't want to encourage a friendship with Vinny Bernard.

The other man shut off his treadmill and looked Lucas over, as if deciding whether or not to push further. "Right. Yeah. My wife is waiting too," he finally said. "Night, man."

"Night."

Bernard walked away, his big body swaying from side to side.

Lucas shook his head and decided he wasn't coming back again without Derek or Kade. Too many weird people in this city.

MAXIE WAS INVITED to go to lunch and costume shopping with Lexie and her sister, Kendall. Knowing that Lucas wasn't into the dressing-up part of the party—something he'd mentioned more than once—she'd agreed to buy the costumes for them both. In exchange, he'd consented to dress up as Batman to her Catwoman.

She and the twins had a nice lunch, and Maxie discovered she liked Kendall as much as she did her sister. The other woman was more subdued than Lexie, and Maxie couldn't help but wonder if her medication kept her on such an even keel. Regardless, she was warm and friendly, and the three of them laughed about the men and their aversion to dressing up. Kendall didn't mention Julian, and Maxie knew better than to bring him up herself.

From lunch, they headed to one of the many costume shops that popped up in Manhattan around Halloween time. The party had been planned for this coming Friday.

Maxie already had a tight pair of black leggings, thigh-high boots, and a tight black scoop-neck top. She'd rather wear her own comfortable clothes than the plastic items that came in one package. What she needed here were the mask and ears, which she easily found. Lucas had made it clear he'd wear his own black pants and top, so she found his accessories as well.

She turned around to find Kendall behind her. "Did you find what you were looking for?" she asked.

Maxie nodded and held up her items. "Did you?"

Kendall smiled. "Harley Quinn at your service." She held up the package with her costume. The picture on the front had short shorts, cropped top, and stadium jacket. "I'm going to dye my hair," she said, excitement in her voice.

"Oh, that's perfect for you," Lexie said, coming up beside them, her hands full.

"What do you have there?" Kendall asked.

"Spiderman and his superhero girlfriend, Black Cat, a.k.a. Felicia Hardy. I have to make my own costume, but I'll wear a blonde wig."

"We'll look similar," Maxie mused. "I haven't gone out and had fun like this in ages. I can't wait."

"I could use a little fun myself," Kendall said. "Except I'll be the single, unattached woman, and I don't think there's anyone at Blink I'll have much in common with."

And that's when Maxie realized Kendall's somber mood might have more to do with Julian… or lack of being coupled up.

"Come on. You don't know that. They're inviting people they work with, so you never know," Lexie said.

Kendall shrugged. "Whatever. Are we ready to head to the register?"

"I am," Maxie said.

Lexie nodded and they headed up front to pay for their costumes.

A little while later, they walked out and stopped on the sidewalk. "So this has been fun, and we're going to have an amazing night," Maxie smiled. Because she was really looking forward to letting loose at a Halloween party with Lucas.

HALLOWEEN WAS IN full force as Maxie and Lucas stepped off the elevator on the executive floor of Blink. Gothic candelabras greeted them. Black cobwebs hung in the corners and across the walls, fake spiders showed up in odd places, and portable strobe lights along with creepy music set the mood.

According to Lexie, Lucas, Kade, and Derek had been generous with the Halloween party plans, providing money and carte blanche for the arrangements. Since they agreed to invite key investors, Lexie had even hired a catering company and a professional to handle the décor.

"Money well spent," Lucas said, nodding his head in approval.

"It does look great. Let's check things out," she said, grasping his hand.

"I feel like an ass," he muttered, obviously hesitant about showing his face in front of his employees. Or his costume, as the case might've been. He'd been complaining while getting dressed.

"Well, you don't look like one." If he'd worn tights, she'd give more credence to his complaint. "You look hot," she assured him.

In his black jeans, turtleneck top, a nice amount of facial scruff, and a mask over his eyes, he was her superhero. Even the bat ears were a fun touch. Though she couldn't deny she'd have preferred to see him in black tights that outlined his delectably large package and spandex showcasing his impressive muscles. Still, she'd take what she could get, and the man made a sexy Batman.

"Actually you're the one who looks hot," he said in a gruff voice.

He turned her toward him and pulled her close. "Those skintight black leggings gave me a hard-on the second you walked out wearing them. This top?" He ran a hand around the outline of her scoop-neck sweater, his calloused touch causing goose bumps on her skin as her nipples hardened painfully. "And I want to fuck you with those thigh-high boots wrapped around my waist."

She shivered with desire, her sex growing heavy and wet. "Lucas," she murmured.

"Tell me you want that too." His dark gaze, surrounded by the mask, bored into hers.

"Of course I want it." Badly.

A grin formed at his lips. "Want what?" He stepped in closer, protecting her from prying eyes, and tweaked a nipple in one hand. "Say it, beautiful."

She all but moaned as sensation struck, shooting from her breasts to her clit. "I want you to fuck me while I'm wearing these boots." Her own words embarrassed her, but Lucas had her beyond reason.

"Later, I promise."

She cleared her throat and took a step back, hoping to clear her mind. "We need to mingle."

"Thank God it's dark or this whole place would know how much I want you."

She laughed but was equally aroused. Still, she pushed the feelings aside for later. "Come on, killjoy. I see Lexie and Spiderman, and if you think you have issues with your costume, go look at your friend."

That instantly cheered Lucas up, because he stopped dragging his feet, and they headed across the room to where Kade was dressed in a red-and-blue one-piece costume with a full headed covering.

"Hi!" Lexie said, her gaze darting from Lucas to Maxie.

"Hi! You look great!" Maxie took in the other woman's white-blonde wig, black mask, her black bustier, and spandex leggings.

"Isn't this fun?" she asked.

"I'm out of here in ten minutes," Kade said, clearly grumpy.

"Can't say I blame you," Lucas said, doing his best not to laugh at his friend.

"Screw it." He pulled the head covering off. "I'm going without this damned thing."

Lexie didn't say a word. She obviously knew her husband had had enough.

"Where's Derek?" Kade asked. "I don't think we should have to suffer alone."

"He left a message with Becky that he had a family crisis and he'd be late."

"Lucky son of a bitch," Lucas said. He scanned the room. "I see Etienne Roberts. Groucho Marx over there. He's a major investor. I think Kade and I should go talk to him for a bit. Can you hold your own here?" he asked Maxie.

"I'm good," she assured him.

He braced a hand on her shoulder, leaned down, and kissed her cheek. "Back in a few minutes."

Kade planted a kiss on Lexie's lips before joining Lucas and heading across the room. "I'd say things are going well," Lexie commented.

"I… I think they are. He's not pressuring me for things I can't handle."

"One day at a time," Lexie said with a smile.

"That's been my motto."

The women stood in silence for a few minutes, then Lexie's face lit up. "Oh! There's Kendall. She didn't want to come early with me to oversee setup. I should go get her. She doesn't know anyone."

"I'm going to take a quick trip to the ladies' room. I can meet up with you later. Can you direct me?"

Lexie pointed across the room. "Over there. In the corner. It's unisex," she explained. "I'll go grab Kendall and get us some punch. Alcohol-free because we wanted to keep things under control."

"Smart," Maxie said. "And punch sounds great. I'll be right back."

She headed for the back corner, smiling at people she didn't know along the way. Just as she reached the bathroom, a large male body blocked her way.

"Excuse me," she said, and tried to step around him, but he continued to prevent her from passing.

"You're Mrs. Monroe," the man said in a vaguely familiar voice.

Nobody had referred to her by her married name since she'd left the firm and changed to her maiden name. And nobody here knew her except Lucas' friends. "Who are you?" she asked.

"You mean you don't recognize me?" He pulled off the mask, and she immediately identified the man. "Vincent Bernardi," she said, a tremor rushing through her at the realization.

"Nice to see you too," he said in a too-pleasant tone.

"What are you doing here?"

He slid the mask back over his eyes before answering. "Well, we both know your husband is a dead end," he said, a combination of sarcasm and anger in his voice. "I sat in prison, chomping at the bit to get what's mine. When I got out, I checked out your storage locker and your old apartment—"

She sucked in a startled breath. "*You* broke in there? *Why?*"

"Because your husband had something that belongs to me, and now that I'm out, I want it back." He met her gaze, his eyes dark behind the mask.

Nausea rose in her throat. "I have no idea what you're looking for."

He studied her, assessing. "For your sake, I hope that's true," he said, the threat in his words and tone clear.

If she'd had any question of his guilt in the assault case—and she didn't—it would have been erased now. The man would do anything he had to in order to get his way.

Panic filled her, and she glanced around, praying Lucas or one of the twins would come looking for her, but other than a man who walked past her and headed straight for the bathroom, ignoring them on his way, she was alone with a man she feared was unhinged.

"It *is* true," she insisted. "I'm clueless about whatever you're looking for."

"Then let me enlighten you. I trusted your husband and gave him something for safekeeping. The information on the memory card I gave him belongs to me. I need it to start over, and you're going to help me find it."

She blew out a deep breath, her insides trembling. Damn, Keith. Would the surprises never end? "Keith's gone. I have no idea where he might have left it."

"Then I suggest you figure it out. Go through the storage unit until you find it. I was interrupted before I could finish the job. Or give me the key, and I'll do a more thorough search—"

"No." She didn't want him going through her things. "I'll look for it." She wanted nothing more than for this man to go away and never return. "But I need time. I can't just come up with this memory card overnight. I've already been through the safe deposit box in both our names, and it wasn't in there."

He studied her. Nodding once, he seemingly accepted her sincerity. She assumed that the reason his anger was under control was because she was cooperating. The thought calmed her, but she was still petrified he would hurt her if she couldn't uncover the stupid memory card. After all, he had gone to jail for assault, and anger management went along with his sentence.

"I'll find you to continue this conversation or hopefully retrieve my property."

She blinked and he was gone, lost in a sea of masks and costumes.

Oh God. She leaned against the nearest wall and attempted to pull herself together. But how could she when Keith's past had come back to bite her yet again? Not only did she have this dangerous man following her, he wanted something desperately. Something she had no idea how to find. And he was capable of extreme brutality when angered.

She choked back a sob.

"Maxie?"

"Lucas!" She threw herself into his arms, letting go with all the panic she'd been feeling.

"Maxie." Lucas grasped her forearms and pulled her back. "What happened?"

She drew in a deep breath. "I was going to the ladies' room, and this guy in a mask confronted me. I remember him. Keith used to represent him, and he recently got out of jail, where he served time for assault."

Lucas ripped the mask off his face and dropped it to the floor. "How the hell did he find you here?"

"Apparently he's been following me." The words made her nauseous.

"What the fuck?" The words exploded from Lucas' mouth.

She swallowed hard. "Keith had something that belongs to him, and he wants it back. He was the one who broke into the storage unit and my old apartment looking, but he didn't find it. And trust me, this isn't the kind of guy you want to cross."

Lucas closed his eyes and visibly drew steadying breaths. "I cannot believe this. That dumb fucking son of a bitch," he said of his brother.

"I know." Maxie couldn't help the wry smile that pulled at her lips. "Keith is the gift that keeps on giving," she muttered.

Lucas choked back a laugh too.

She sobered quickly though. "Somehow I have to figure out where he would have hidden something small. It was a flash drive that has information that belongs to this Vincent Bernardi."

"Wait. Vincent Bernardi." He repeated the name and paused, obviously thinking hard.

"What is it? Do you know him?" she asked.

Lucas narrowed his gaze. "Last week I was at the

gym, and a guy named Vinny Bernard cornered me. He tried to get friendly, asking questions about the area. He said he was new to town. But then he asked if I had a brother, and he started rambling about his. I got an uneasy vibe, and I left the gym. What does Bernardi look like?"

She swallowed hard. "He's big. Unusually so. Black hair. But he was wearing a mask at first. After that it was dark. I can't describe him well, but I'd recognize him again."

"Well, big describes the guy I met too." Lucas frowned. "The son of a bitch tried to get friendly with me. So he could get near my things so he could search? Or see if I gave up information about Keith?" He shook his head, unable to figure out the man's end game.

Maxie only knew he wanted something he believed she had. "I have to tear the storage unit apart." Her voice shook, and he pulled her against him.

"You aren't alone. We'll figure out what to do. One step at a time," he reassured her.

And for the first time, she wasn't in such a rush to go out and handle things all on her own.

WHILE MAXIE SLEPT, Lucas held her close and stared up at the ceiling. His brother's behavior defied description or logic. Every time Lucas thought he'd heard the worst, Keith sank lower. Anger swirled in his gut, but once again it was a useless feeling. There was nothing he could do to change the past, Keith's behavior, or the fact that he was gone and Lucas couldn't confront him. Nor could he maintain the level of anger and frustration boiling inside him while he was around Maxie.

Tomorrow he and Maxie would go through her storage locker with a fine-tooth comb. He'd also put security on Maxie and his parents. He didn't trust that this Vincent Bernardi character wouldn't go after his parents or break into their house looking for the media card. Lucas frowned as a thought crossed his mind.

Could Keith have somehow hidden the card in Lucas' apartment? His brother hadn't come up here often, but he had been here. And nobody had more flash drives lying around than Lucas.

He rolled over and quietly slipped out of bed, heading for the corner room, where he had his home office. He started going through his drawers, pulling out spare storage drives and slipping them into his laptop, running a quick check on the contents, one after another, coming up empty each time. He had old information of his own but nothing that didn't belong to him.

He ran a hand through his hair and laughed at

himself. What were the chances his brother would toss an important drive among Lucas' things, where it could get thrown out? Slim to none, but he'd be negligent if he didn't at least check. And Lucas had spare flash drives everywhere in his office.

Thirty minutes later, he had a pile of USB drives, and he hadn't gotten anywhere in his search. But he still had to protect his family.

Grabbing his cell phone, he walked into the darkened living room. The only lights were the windows from other buildings across the way and New York City.

He dialed Kade, who picked up on the first ring. "Hey, man. You left the party early. Everything okay?"

Lucas stared out the window into the night. "I'll explain soon. In the meantime, your friend Ian Dare, the one who invested in Blink…" Ian and Kade had been friends in college, meeting after Lucas dropped out. "Didn't you once say he had a brother with a top-notch security firm?"

"Yes. Tyler Dare. He co-owns Double Down Security with his brother, Scott. They're based in Miami, but I'm sure they can either send you someone or hook you up with a reputable firm here. You sure you don't want to tell me what's going on?"

"Later. I need to make some arrangements first, but thanks."

"Any time. I'll text you the number as soon as we hang up."

Lucas disconnected the call with Kade and put in a call to Double Down Security. With a little luck, he'd have security on the people he loved by morning.

He stopped short at his choice of words, then realized he shouldn't be surprised. He'd loved Maxie for a long time. Granted, it hadn't been the same kind of love he felt for her now. When he was younger, he'd had a crush, then as they got older, he'd idolized her. Considered her out of his league as any more than a friend. Then they'd grown apart, and though he'd held on to the adoration he'd felt for her, the truth was he hadn't really known Maxie, the woman she'd become. And once his brother moved in, Lucas had taken an even bigger step back, both mentally and emotionally. He'd always been there for her, but they hadn't connected.

Lucas truly believed that now they were living their time. And he didn't want anything getting in the way. Which meant he also had to sit his parents down and make sure they understood exactly who their other son had been. And why they had to leave Lucas and Maxie alone.

THE STORAGE UNIT was still in upheaval from Bernardi's search. Maxie hadn't had time to clean up the mess the first time she visited, so she and Lucas worked for hours righting things and searching everything they could for a small flash drive.

It wasn't easy to keep her anger, frustration, and hurt at bay during the long morning. All aimed at the crazy man she'd married. She closed up a box that contained Keith's personal effects from his nightstand drawer, once again not coming up with the elusive flash drive. She probably ought to be afraid, but with Lucas by her side, she didn't allow that emotion to surface. She'd worry about Vincent Bernardi later.

"You know," she said to Lucas, "I packed Keith's stuff up for a reason. It's not like I want to be looking through his papers and personal effects. I was planning to give your mom a key when she was ready and let your parents decide what to keep and what to get rid of."

Lucas placed a hand over hers. "I'm sorry you have to go through this."

She smiled wryly. "It's definitely not your fault. And I appreciate your help." She didn't know what she'd have done without him.

"When are you going to realize I'd do anything for you?" he asked.

He'd made that comment at other times in the past, but something in his brown eyes and intense expression was different now. More protective. Possessive.

Before she could figure out what, he continued. "And because I'd do anything for you, I have some things I'd like to talk to you about, and after a morning doing this, you're not going to like it."

"Spit it out. I'm not sure there's much more that can shock me."

He nodded. "I hired security to protect you. I don't trust this Bernardi character, and I'm worried about him coming near you again."

She blew out a long breath. "And you're expecting me to be upset that you're making decisions for me or taking over my life?"

"Something like that."

She stood and walked over to the box on which he sat, rested her head on his shoulder.

Exhaustion overwhelmed her but he was her rock. "I'm not upset. I'm so grateful that you care enough to keep me safe. I can be stubborn but I'm not stupid."

He laughed and breathed out an obvious sigh of relief. "Well, that went easier than I thought. Next I have to deal with my parents."

She looked up and met his gaze. "Have you heard from them?"

He shook his head. "But I need to go see them."

"Okay … they're your parents. You should visit

with them." But there was something he wasn't saying. "Lucas, what's wrong?"

"I hired people to protect them too. What if Bernardi starts to think maybe Keith gave the flash drive to my mother or father for safekeeping? He could go after them." Lucas clenched his hands into fists.

"Oh my God. Do you think Keith did?" Maxie asked, horrified by the notion.

"Everything inside me wants to say no. He wouldn't involve my parents, but if you'd asked me six months ago, I wouldn't have thought he'd involve you."

He had a point, Maxie thought.

"So I have to go tell them everything. They need to know exactly how bad things were with their son so they can be prepared and safe."

And after the reaction they'd had about Keith last time Lucas had tried to talk to them, he must be dreading the confrontation.

She cupped his face in her hand. "I'm sorry *you* have to go through this."

"It's definitely not your fault either." His lips twisted in a wry grin.

"I know your parents aren't thrilled with us right now, but I'd be happy to go with you. For moral support."

His eyes glittered with admiration. Considering her

freak out after her in-laws had discovered her living with Lucas, she understood his reaction.

"Thank you but I need to do this myself. And it's not going to be pleasant, so I think you should stay home."

"I respect that," she murmured. Everyone had things they needed to accomplish on their own, and just because she was allowing for security and help didn't mean she'd changed her mind about the need to be independent. She was just taking a few detours on the road to getting there.

They returned to their search for another hour, until finally Lucas spoke from across the unit. "Well, this place seems like a dead end," Lucas said.

Her stomach flipped, knowing that was not a good thing. "Maybe there is something at your parents', or what about Keith's old office?" she asked hopefully.

"It's been awhile, but we could ask if there were any personal effects they didn't pass on to you."

Maxie nodded, grasping on to any hope that they could find what Bernardi wanted and get him out of her life once and for all.

"Are you ready to get out of here? I could stand to eat lunch."

No sooner had he asked the question than her stomach growled in response.

She laughed. "That answers your question. Just

one more thing." Her gaze fell to the one box she hadn't opened.

"What's that?" he asked, his stare following hers.

"It's got some things in it that were meant for the baby." She wrapped her arms around herself. "I couldn't bring myself to part with them, so I hid them in my closet."

He closed his eyes and shook his head. "Why hide it? I'm almost afraid to ask."

She swallowed hard. "Keith got rid of anything related to the baby immediately, so I stashed things I couldn't bear to part with at the bottom of my closet. One night when he was out, I packed it all into a box and put it beneath old sweaters." She shrugged. "They were the only links I had to the life that grew inside me."

"Aww. C'mere." He held out his arms and she walked into them.

When she was enveloped in his embrace and the comforting smell of everything that was Lucas, the pain and sadness that came with the memories weren't quite as sharp and acute. She rested her head against his chest, listening to the steady beat of his heart and letting it soothe her.

"I want to take the box home. If Bernardi comes back, I don't want anything that has special meaning to be left for him to tear apart." She tipped her head up and looked at him.

"Whatever you want."

She smiled. "Thank you."

He tapped her on the nose. "Thanking me is unnecessary. Let's get going. I'll put the box in the car and we can feed you."

She knew he was deliberately lightening the mood, and she appreciated it. "Me? You're the one who said you were hungry." She stepped back, giving him room so he could lift the box.

"And you're the one with the noisy stomach."

She couldn't argue with that. So she pulled out the keys to the unit and locked things up behind them, leaving Keith's things where they belonged. Unfortunately, his legacy still followed her... and would until she found that flash drive.

Chapter Nine

LUCAS PULLED UP to the standard colonial in a Long Island suburb he'd bought his parents after Blink took off. They'd been hesitant about moving, but their old house was in need of serious repair, and Lucas had talked them into moving. He'd called ahead to make sure they'd both be home, and as he pulled into the driveway, he caught sight of the car idling a few feet away, a man keeping an eye on the house. It wasn't much, but he had Bernardi's description. Hopefully he wouldn't get by the detail.

He rang the doorbell, but when he turned the knob, it opened easily. Something that would change once his parents became aware of the threat.

"Mom? Dad?" Lucas called out as he stepped inside, shut the door, and turned the lock.

"In the kitchen," his mother replied.

Lucas walked down a short hall and turned into

the room. His father sat at the table drinking his coffee. His mother, it seemed, had just poured herself a cup.

"Lucas, can I get you something?"

He shook his head. "I came to talk."

"Son, I'm not sure this is the right time," his father said. Obviously he knew the direction of the conversation Lucas wanted to have.

"There's never going to be a right time, and now it can't wait."

"Why?" his mother asked. "Why can't we leave your brother's indiscretions in the past?"

His frustration with his parents' denial grew. "Because they were more than indiscretions," Lucas said through clenched teeth. "Let me put it to you this way. A guy threatened Maxie if she doesn't turn over something that Keith had of his. And she doesn't know what he's talking about. He already broke into her storage unit and old apartment. And I can't guarantee he won't come after you two or break in here looking for it, so I hired protection."

His mother gasped and his father blanched. He walked over and put an arm around his wife's shoulders. "Lucas—"

"No joke, Dad. There's a security guard sitting outside. So if you two don't want to hear about your angel son, fine. Just make sure you lock the doors and set the alarm." Lucas dug into his pocket and pulled out a business card. "And if you have a problem, call this number. The guy outside will be here in seconds." He slapped the card on the table.

He'd done what he could, protected his family despite their stubborn refusal to see the truth.

"Did Keith give you anything for safekeeping?" Lucas asked.

"No," his father said.

He glanced at his mother, who shook her head, obviously too upset to speak.

"Is there any place Keith could have hidden it here?" he asked.

"Your brother didn't come out to visit," his father admitted. "We had to go to the city if we wanted to see him."

Lucas blew out a frustrated breath. "What about anything odd? Did anyone approach you? A big man who liked to talk a lot?" He described Bernardi in further detail.

"That sounds like the new exterminator," his mother said. "He showed up one morning and said Ralph, our regular man, was out sick. He talked a lot about his son and how hard it was when a kid was a disappointment."

Which was how he'd tried to play Lucas, discussing brothers, hoping he'd open up. With his parents, he'd discussed a son. "Did you engage with him?" Lucas asked.

She frowned and shook her head. "He annoyed me, and I cut him off to make a phone call."

Lucas leaned against the counter. "Did he have free reign of the house after that?"

She nodded. "Exterminators always do."

"And did you notice anything out of place after he left?"

She pursed her lips and grew quiet, thinking. "Now that you mention it, I had to go into all the rooms he'd been in to shut the lights. Ralph always remembers to do that himself. And there were some open drawers, but I assumed the cleaning lady had been dusting and left them ajar."

Lucas groaned. So Bernardi had been here and found nothing. Chances were he wouldn't be back, but security would make sure of it.

"From now on, set the alarm and call me or the security company if something seems out of the ordinary."

"I will," his mother said, sounding grateful.

"Fine. I'm going to get going." Lucas had said all he'd come to say.

He didn't want to believe his father was choosing sides between his children, but his inability to see the bad in Keith left Lucas feeling less than. Something he was damned tired of dealing with in his life. And something he was long past. Except when it came to his parents.

Lucas turned to leave when his father spoke. "Son… there's more I need to say."

Lucas paused mid-step and turned, facing his dad.

He realized his father was still suffering, the lines around his eyes so pronounced. Despite everything, it hurt Lucas to see. He waited for the older man to speak.

"I knew your brother didn't have your moral fiber. Or mine," he finally said, the admission taking Lucas by surprise.

His father grabbed on to the back of a chair as he spoke. "We thought Maxie would be a good influence on him. You were in California when they started to date and… we hoped he'd stop looking for more, for better—"

"For what I had? Or wanted?" Lucas asked, unable to hide the bitterness in his tone. "Or was that something you conveniently shut your eyes to as well?"

His father looked away. His mother hadn't lifted her gaze from her lap. "You were smart. Such a good boy. We knew only great things would come your way. Your brother? He tried too hard, and we thought once you left, he'd mellow out. He always was too competitive."

Lucas' mouth turned dry at that convoluted way of seeing the past. "Are you saying I had it easy? I was bullied by Keith and his friends. School was hard because I couldn't sit still. I was smart but it was too simplistic, too easy. Dropping out wasn't easy. I felt like a failure, while Keith was the golden boy. Your favorite by far, popular, sports star, and yet there was nothing I could have that he didn't try to take away. Maxie was his ultimate *screw you* to me. And you stood by and let it happen because you were more worried about Keith!" Lucas exploded, the words flying from his mouth in a torrent of held-back pain and rage.

"Because if we didn't, we had to face our failures as parents!" his father exploded in return.

"So instead you sacrificed me." Lucas felt sick.

Bryce winced. "We didn't know Keith was so mentally sick or how far he'd go to get what he wanted."

Maybe you should have paid more attention. Yet despite Lucas' disappointment in his parents, he couldn't bring himself to hurt them by saying those thoughts out loud.

"Well, he *was* sick and he did a lot of damage. Especially to Maxie. And that's the other reason I came. I'm not sure where things are headed with us, but I know where I want things to go." And he was bringing her there at her own pace. "But if Maxie and I do end up together, and you can't give your blessing, you need to say nothing at all. She doesn't deserve your disapproval. Not after all Keith put her through." He met his father's stare with a challenging one of his own.

Let him think about all he'd said today and come to terms. Or not. Nothing would change how Lucas felt about Maxie or what he wanted for their future.

FOR THE FIRST time since starting work, Maxie called in sick. She woke up queasy, which turned into real nausea. She figured she had picked up a virus similar to the one Lexie had had a week or so before. Instead of pushing herself to try and get into the office, she took the day off.

It didn't help that she was in a complete panic because, to date, they hadn't found the USB drive Vincent Bernardi wanted, and she didn't know if they ever would.

At the thought, she ran for the bathroom and emptied what little she'd been able to eat this morning. She washed up and brushed her teeth, then returned to the family room to rest on the couch.

As for Bernardi, she couldn't forget him because he was always around. He didn't approach her, her security guard made certain of that, but she'd noticed him outside her place of work during the day and hanging near their apartment building in the evening.

She ran into him at a coffee shop, where he merely nodded at her with a knowing smile. His obvious intent was to let her know he wasn't going anywhere… and she owed him his property.

While home for the day, she looked through all her personal things again just in case Keith had put the flash drive in, say, her jewelry box, but nothing there.

Before coming home from work, Lucas had gone to meet with Julian Dane, fulfilling his promise to Kade to make sure he steered clear of Kendall. She wondered how that meeting was going. He'd had a lot of stress in his life lately, and she'd done what she could to soothe him at home.

He hadn't talked much about his conversation with his mother and father, but he wasn't happy with them. She knew what it was like to be estranged from your parents. Her father had never bothered with her, not even as a child. And she and her mother had so little in common they couldn't be in the same room without her mother criticizing everything about Maxie's life. Over time, she'd found it easier not to have much to do with her at all.

But that wasn't how Lucas lived his life. For all his family's flaws, he loved them. She hoped that over time they'd accept the truth about Keith and open their hearts to the son they had left.

She shut the television and straightened up the

family room, then returned to her bedroom to grab clean pajamas, shower, and change for bed. She'd been sleeping in Lucas' room and had no desire to change things. She'd grown used to being wrapped in his arms, and she even admitted to herself that he'd done everything in his power to allow her the independence she needed. She wasn't looking to the future, but now was pretty damned good.

Her gaze fell to the box she'd left in the corner. The baby's items from the storage unit, a distinct reminder of the past. The painful lump immediately formed in her chest.

Maybe it was time to let these items go. She couldn't rewind events and change the outcome, and she needed to be able to enjoy the life she'd created and was living now. Every time she caught sight of the box, she was dragged back into suffocating memories. They'd always be with her, but she couldn't deny that getting rid of the box was a symbol of being ready to move on.

She sat down on the floor and opened the flaps on top. First she pulled out the soft blue blanket with a satin fringe. She rubbed the gentle material against her cheek, closed her eyes, and allowed herself to shed a tear for what she'd lost. And what she decided she'd never have. She couldn't imagine taking that risk ever again. Not when the agony of the loss was so acute and the spiral of depression had been so deep.

She opened her eyes and folded the blanket. Next came the little bear she'd found in a department store baby department. She touched her nose to the stuffed animal and smiled, putting it on top of the blanket. Next came the mobile. Blue and yellow in color, it had plastic arms from which hung adorable baby sheep. Without batteries, the music didn't work, but she'd been so excited to use it.

She lifted it into the air, and one arm fell off, revealing a hollow inside. She picked up the piece, intending to insert it back into the main mobile, when a small blue chip fell out of the hollow arm and dropped to the floor.

She blinked, disbelieving what was right in front of her eyes. "It can't be."

She picked up the item and held it in the air. Sure enough, it was a flash drive.

"That son of a bitch!" He'd known she kept the baby stuff all along. He must have known she never opened that box, the memories too painful, so he'd stashed Bernardi's information where nobody would ever think to look. A place that was sacred to Maxie... but why would Keith care about her feelings at all? He'd put on such a big show about her getting rid of everything related to the baby, she'd never, ever think he knew about this box or go into it if he had.

But his death had left her holding the proverbial ball, and in his arrogance, he'd never planned for that eventuality at all. The selfish bastard. She packed up the box of items, planning to donate them to Goodwill. And with the drive in hand, she waited for Lucas to come home.

LUCAS WALKED INTO the restaurant where he was due to meet with Julian. Before the settlement meetings over Blink, Lucas hadn't seen the man in years. Even when he was involved in the early stages of development, Julian had begun to move in groups that partied far more heavily than Kade and Derek's friends.

He caught sight of Julian waiting at the bar, and he gestured as he walked past the hostess stand.

He and Julian exchanged formal hellos, and Lucas settled into a seat next to him.

Julian looked healthy. His dark hair was cut short, his eyes clear. No sign of any drug use as far as Lucas could tell. Not that he was an expert.

"I've been clean for years," Julian said as if reading Lucas' mind.

He didn't have any reason to doubt him. "Glad to hear it."

"So what can I do for you?" Julian asked. "You called this meeting."

The bartender strode over and placed a napkin in front of each of them. "Can I get you anything?" he asked.

"No thank you," Lucas said. He wanted to get this conversation over with. A drink was the last thing on his mind.

Julian shook his head. "Nothing for me either, thanks."

Once the bartender made his way to another set of customers, Lucas leaned an arm on the bar and got down to business.

"You need to stay away from Kendall," he said to Julian. "Don't ask about her, and for God's sake, don't make contact with her."

Julian narrowed his gaze. "Kade needs you to talk for him now?" he asked, his face turning an angry red.

"No. I'm here on my own, because if I let Kade do the talking, he'll do it with his fists." Lucas leaned closer. "Look, Julian, you used that girl. Worse, she's got her own issues, and you didn't give a shit."

Julian flinched and Lucas knew he'd taken a direct hit.

"I own what I did to Kendall, and I'm fucking sorry for it. I didn't know about her problems though."

Lucas raised an eyebrow. "And that makes it okay?"

"No. I just said as much." Julian frowned. "You

don't like me and that's fine. But we both know I was entitled to the settlement I received from Blink. You guys were going to throw everything you could at me to cut me out. I did what I had to do. For many reasons, none of which I plan to explain to you."

Great. So where did they stand? Lucas wondered. "So what do you want? What was that visit about the other day?"

Julian set his jaw, his tension obvious.

"I regret hurting Kendall, and I want to know that she's okay. I *need* to know."

Lucas recognized Julian's expression and uttered a silent, resounding curse in his head. He saw that look on Kade's face when he talked about Lexie. He'd probably see it in his own gaze when he looked at Maxie. Which meant that unless Julian agreed to leave Kendall alone, none of them were finished with Julian in their lives.

Lucas straightened his shoulders and tried again to make his point. "The best thing for everyone is if you live your own life. Far away from any of us. Including and especially Kendall."

Julian winced and Lucas wondered if he'd actually hurt the man's feelings.

"Kendall is doing well," Lucas heard himself saying, the words unplanned. He hadn't intended to give Julian any information on the woman he'd used for financial gain.

Julian let out a long, relieved breath. "Thank you."

"Don't thank me. That's all you're getting from me. Not another piece of information, so don't ask. Don't snoop around. And for the love of God, don't provoke Kade."

"You guys are lucky to have held on to your friendship all these years," Julian said.

Lucas merely nodded. The other man obviously had more than his share of regrets. Anything Lucas said would only rub salt in a still very open wound. And despite the lawsuit and their rocky past, it wasn't in Lucas' nature to want to hurt the man on purpose.

He wrapped things up with Julian, uncomfortable that he couldn't tell Kade the man was out of his or Kendall's life.

He headed home, satisfied he'd at least put Julian on notice. It was all he could do.

He hoped Maxie would be up waiting for him, but at the very least, he knew she'd be in his bed. More than progress, he thought. The beginning of a life together.

He walked into the apartment, surprised when Maxie practically greeted him at the door. "How are you feeling?" he asked.

"Mostly better. But forget about that. I thought you'd never get home, and I didn't want to call and ask you to leave your meeting with Julian." She bounced up and down in obvious excitement.

"What's going on?" He tossed his keys aside and kicked off his shoes.

"This!" She held out a tiny blue drive. "Look what I found!"

"Holy shit, is that Bernardi's?"

"Well, I didn't check it because I don't have the right computer, but what else would the bastard have hidden in the arm of my baby mobile?" She raised an eyebrow as if daring him to doubt her conclusion.

He plucked the drive from her hand. "I'm sure you're right. But let's find out for certain." Heart pounding with the possibility that the nightmare could be over, he headed to his office and turned on his computer.

He inserted a card reader and put the USB drive in. He clicked a few buttons and brought up the information on the drive. Names and numbers came up on the screen.

"It's a string of symbols and numbers," Lucas said and ejected the drive. "That's all we need to know. No confessions here that we need to feel guilty about. The bastard can have his drive and get out of our lives."

"Thank God," she murmured.

"Considering he's been hanging around, it shouldn't be too hard for me to do a handoff tomorrow." Lucas palmed the small item in his hand.

She cleared her throat, and he looked up, meeting her gaze. "For *who* to do a handoff tomorrow?" she pointedly asked, her gaze serious and intent on his.

He caught on to her meaning immediately. And though he didn't like the idea of bringing her with him to meet with Bernardi, he understood. She had the biggest stake in this situation. Bernardi had come to her directly. And she had a right to handle things in her own life.

So as much as he'd rather be the big bad protector, he pushed back those caveman instincts. "*We* will do the hand-off," he amended.

A bright smile took hold of her face.

"How the hell did you find it?" he asked.

She drew in a deep breath. "I was thinking about where I am in life, and how I was feeling… and I decided it was time to get rid of the box of baby things."

He'd seen her reaction to the box and knew how much the items inside meant to her, what they represented, both in terms of pain and lost hope. He admired her bravery and didn't want to push for answers as to why. It was enough for him that she was ready to move on.

"I wanted to look through them one more time. And when I picked up the mobile, the arm fell off and the drive fell out. It was just that simple. Keith must have figured I'd never open the box or look inside. Can you imagine how unfeeling and callous he had to be to hide something in a box of precious things?" She shook her head, her disbelief as strong as his.

"I don't think we'll ever understand anything my brother did."

She nodded. "I think if the day came when I did, I'd scare myself."

He laughed. "Well, tomorrow we can send Bernardi on his way. Tonight, we celebrate."

MAXIE THOUGHT CELEBRATING was a fine idea. All she had to do was look at Lucas and her body softened, desire sweeping through her. From the heated look in his eyes, he wanted her too, and she was on board.

He plunged his hand into her hair and pulled her against him, his lips coming down on hers.

She moaned and wrapped her arms around his neck, the kiss one of mutual need and growing hunger. He nipped at her bottom lip, then slid his tongue inside, tangling with hers. He dominated her with his big hand in her hair, and she clung to him, her breasts pressed against his chest, desire pulsing through her core. Her heart beat out a rapid rhythm as she lost sense of time and place. Nothing existed but Lucas and the depth of need he both pulled from inside her and also exhibited with this one kiss.

With a low growl, he broke the kiss, picked her up, and carried her to his bedroom. "This caveman side of you turns me on," she said, rubbing her cheek against his roughened one.

"Good to know." He deposited her on the bed and stripped off his clothes. She wriggled out of her pajamas and leaned back against the mattress and pillows, waiting.

He grabbed a condom and tossed it onto the bed. Then his gaze locked on hers, sliding from her face, down her naked body, his gaze darkening with pure need.

Feeling emboldened by the look in his eyes, she bent one knee, exposing herself to his view.

He wrapped a hand around his cock, pumping from base to tip and back again. "You're so fucking beautiful."

Her body was already on fire, and her heart melted at his words. "Come here," she whispered.

He slid onto the bed beside her, his erection gliding over her hip, the tip dampening her skin. He pressed a soft kiss to her collarbone, licking her flesh, working his way lower, until he reached her full breasts.

He cupped one in his hand and pulled her nipple into his mouth, suckling on the sensitive tip until her hips rose on the bed, an aching emptiness between her thighs.

He braced one hand on her lower belly, holding her down, and continued teasing the tight bud, first one nipple, then the other, until she was writhing and moaning with unrestrained need.

"You aren't playing fair," she said on a shaky breath.

"Just taking my time and enjoying." He kissed the tip of one breast, then the other, then moved lower, his lips trailing a moist path directly to her sex.

"Lucas," she groaned.

"Taking my time," he reminded her, his mouth coming down directly on her sex, his tongue sliding over her outer lips.

"Oh God."

He chuckled, his warm breath continuing his deliberately playful arousal. And he didn't pause in his ministrations. He licked, teased, nipped, and soothed his way around her pussy. He speared her body with his tongue, and she arched her hips in a futile attempt to pull him deeper inside her.

She grasped his hair and held his face down, unable to stop herself as she ground herself against his mouth. And he continued to devour her without stopping, until her climax hit hard, taking her up and over the peak. Wave after wave of pleasure swept through her, and his mouth latched on to her clit as she came, the orgasm seeming to go on forever.

She finally collapsed against the bed in a spent heap. Until she heard the sound of the condom wrapper crinkling, and her body came alive once more.

She opened her eyes just as Lucas came over her, his large body dwarfing hers, his huge erection poised at her entrance.

"I dream about you, open for me just like this."

Her cheeks flushed at his frank talk. "Lucas."

"Yes, beautiful. It's me." And as he spoke, he thrust deep, his solid erection taking her, *owning* her as he pulsed inside her.

His gaze met hers, warm and full of emotion, as he slid out slowly, her inner walls feeling every hard ridge and solid inch of his erection, before pushing back inside her completely.

"How is it you're so fucking tight every time? You feel so good, so perfect for me."

Her heart quivered, and emotion lodged in her throat, his words as potent and heartfelt as the feel of his body inside hers.

Instead of picking up the pace and taking her hard, he opted for a slow, rocking motion inside her, his stare hot and serious on hers.

With every roll of his hips against hers, a delicious quaking began to overtake her body. "Oh God, Lucas," she cried out, her fingers digging into his shoulders.

"I feel it too," he assured her, his hands braced on the mattress, his hips in charge of her pleasure... and his, if the low groan from his chest and the tight pull of his lips were any indication.

His hips began a steady thrusting that sent her spiraling higher and higher until her orgasm hit, her body soaring outside itself, pleasure all she knew.

He let go then, a steady series of thrusts continuing the bliss that had overtaken her until he came with a groan, pumping into her over and over until he collapsed on top of her, his cheek nestled against hers, his breath rough and hard in her ear.

"I love you, Maxie."

Her heart squeezed in her chest, and she couldn't have stopped the words that followed if she wanted to. "I love you too, Lucas."

"Thank fuck."

Somehow she laughed, even as she shoved at his shoulders. "I can't breathe."

He pushed himself up and off her, rolling to the side, facing her. "You can't take it back."

She bit the inside of her cheek. "Who says I want to?" she asked.

But she couldn't stop the feeling of panic filling her chest, practically suffocating her. Because the last time she'd given herself up to this feeling of happiness, she'd been pregnant, and it had been cruelly taken away from her. And no matter how much love she felt for this man, she didn't trust the feeling. Not for an instant.

Chapter Ten

M AXIE WOKE UP queasy again, but today she ignored the nausea as best she could, focusing instead on the plan to get rid of the flash drive. She and Lucas hoped Vincent Bernardi would be waiting outside as he had been most mornings. With luck, this was the last time they'd see the man again. She gathered her courage as she dressed for work, admitting that the bulk of her bravery stemmed from the fact that she wouldn't be alone when she faced Bernardi. Lucas would be by her side.

And to his credit, he didn't try and convince her to let him handle the handoff on his own despite his feelings on the matter. Her respect for him multiplied each time he allowed her the space to grow and to be herself. Each time he proved how different he was from his brother.

She couldn't deny she loved the man. Considering

the depth of her feelings for him for years, she hadn't had a long way to fall. Trusting the feelings was another story, but all she could do was take things one day at a time and hope nothing happened to cause a seismic shift in the happiness she was currently experiencing.

"Ready?" Lucas asked as they met up at the front door.

"As I'll ever be." She held out the USB drive.

He eyed it warily but didn't ask for her to hand it over to him. Hands linked, they took the elevator downstairs and stepped out into the bright sunshine of the cool November day. The man Lucas had hired as security stood in his dark glasses by the revolving door to the building.

Maxie shaded her eyes and looked down the street while Lucas glanced in the opposite direction.

"Figures. No sign of Bernardi," she muttered.

"There's always this afternoon," Lucas said, sounding as frustrated as she felt.

He pulled his car keys from his pocket. "Let's go back inside and get my car." They'd need to take the elevator down to the parking garage below street level.

Lucas nodded to the security guard, and he turned to follow them inside.

Maxie took one last look down the street as Vincent Bernardi strode out of the market on the corner.

"Lucas, wait. There he is." She pointed directly at the big man, her stomach turning over as he met her gaze and started walking toward them.

Lucas put up a hand, indicating the security guard shouldn't step in.

"Are you looking for me?" Bernardi said as he walked up to them, coffee in hand.

"Possibly. First I want to know what your plan is once you have what you came for," Lucas said.

Maxie was only too happy to let him lead the exchange. She wanted to be here in person. She didn't care if she ever spoke to the man again.

Bernardi frowned. "None of your damned business. I'm assuming from the way you were looking around for me that you have my property?" He glanced at Maxie.

She straightened her shoulders and nodded. "I found the flash drive."

He extended his arm palm up. "Hand it over."

Lucas stepped forward, pushing Maxie away from him. "First I want your word we'll never see you again."

Bernardi let out a chilling laugh. "That's your issue? Man, hand it over and I'm out of your life for good."

She shoved her hand into her pants pocket and pulled out the drive, smacking it into his beefy hand.

He accepted the drive and walked away. Out of their lives for good.

A WEEK HAD passed since Maxie had turned the flash drive over to Vincent Bernardi. She couldn't help but keep a lookout, check all the usual corners and places he'd been lurking. But no one was around, no tail, no big man making his presence known. He had kept his promise and disappeared.

Still, Lucas had kept the security detail on Maxie and his family through last night, until he finally felt comfortable letting them go, and she appreciated him being extra cautious. But she could finally breathe easily on that score, at least.

There was another matter that had her completely panicked, and she'd had a very difficult time hiding her emotions from Lucas. But tonight he'd gone to the gym with Derek and Kade, so she stopped at the drugstore on the way home and bought a pregnancy test. Panic didn't begin to describe the feelings swirling inside her, from the butterflies in her stomach to the actual nausea still plaguing her to sheer fear.

She didn't want to be pregnant. She was petrified of going through another almost full term, getting attached to the life inside her, only to lose everything to something beyond her control. To be plunged into the black hole of depression once more.

Alone in the bathroom, she pulled out the box with shaking hands and proceeded to follow directions, although she'd done this before. She knew it was smarter to take the test in the morning, but she was alone tonight, so she was going to get this over with. She'd been nauseous long enough, her breasts hurt, and she just had a gut feeling. Still, she needed confirmation before she fell apart.

The waiting took forever. She couldn't even kill time online on her cell phone, checking the clock every few seconds.

Finally, the timer went off.

With her heart in her throat, she looked at the stick. She'd purchased the brand that said Pregnant or Not Pregnant instead of a thin blue line to confirm. So when she glanced at the test, there was no doubt. No question.

She was pregnant.

The damned condom had failed her. She put her face in her hands and cried. After the day of worrying and working herself up for this moment, she needed the release.

What a freaking mess. She was just getting her life together after Keith had destroyed the reality she'd known. She had no savings, a job that needed her to be present and focused, and her push for being independent felt like a big fat sham. Because she was tied to another man because of a baby. Except she loved Lucas. It wasn't his fault she was in no mental state to handle a pregnancy or a baby.

God, what was she going to do?

She wrapped the box and stick in the brown bag and buried it in the kitchen garbage before heading back to the bathroom. She washed her face and patted her burning eyes, staring at her face in the mirror, wondering why things couldn't go her way for once.

Her cell rang and she glanced down. Lexie's name flashed on the screen. She sighed, cleared her throat, and answered. "Hello?"

"Maxie, it's Lexie."

"And Kendall," another voice added into the phone.

"Hi," she said, smiling despite the despair she was feeling. "What's up?"

"Since Kade is out, Kendall and I decided to go out for dinner. We want you to join us," Lexie said.

She really wasn't in the mood to go out and be with people. On the other hand, she didn't want to sit home and dwell either. She had decisions to make, but none had to be made tonight.

"Where are you going?" Maxie asked.

A half an hour later, she'd pulled herself together, put on some makeup, and headed out to meet the twins at a restaurant near her apartment. Because the location wasn't far, she decided a walk would clear her head. The last thing she needed was for Lucas to come home to find her with a blotchy face and red eyes and ask questions. She needed time, and keeping busy tonight would buy her some.

She walked out the building's front door and into the cool evening air, feeling better as soon as the air hit her face. There was something refreshing about an outdoor walk, and if she was lucky, a miracle answer would dawn on her.

She drew her jacket around her and started down the street. As she passed the corner mini-mart, a man called her name.

She turned to see Vincent Bernardi quickly catching up with her. Her heart began to race. "What are you doing here?"

He grasped her elbow. "Keep walking," he said, pulling her along at a steady clip.

"I thought you said you'd leave me alone."

"Lady, you're trying my patience, and I don't have much to begin with." Instead of heading straight on the well-lit avenue, he turned into a more dimly lit side street.

Her mouth went dry, and her nausea kicked in again for reasons beyond being pregnant.

"Took me awhile to check all my accounts and stay

under the radar, but my funds are missing. Which means either you or your douchebag husband stole my money."

She dug her heels into the sidewalk and stopped walking. "What? I didn't even know there were accounts on that drive! I mean, if I were going to take your money, I wouldn't still be here, would I? I'd be long gone!"

"I don't give a fuck if it was you or your husband. It was mine and I want it back." He still held on to her elbow and shook her hard, displaying his infamous temper, and her insides shook with fear. "Lucky for you, your boyfriend is rich. He can repay what his fucking brother stole from me."

"I—" She didn't have an answer to that. How could she ask Lucas to step up and pay for his brother's sins?

"Take my number." He slipped her a piece of paper. "You have one week, or I'll be back, and you won't like what happens if I have to contact you again," he said, and she knew he meant business.

LUCAS SAT WITH Kade and Derek, having a drink before heading home for the night. All in all, things were going well. Business was on track, new development and improvements in the works, and things at home with Maxie were progressing at a pace he could more than live with. Even his asshole brother's mess was behind them.

They'd just paid the bill when Kade's phone rang. "Yeah, baby?"

Derek rolled his eyes, and Lucas couldn't wait until he was on the receiving end of wanting to get home to his woman.

"What? I'll tell him and I'll see you soon. Love you."

"What's up?" Lucas asked.

Kade's brows furrowed. "Lexie and Kendall were supposed to meet Maxie for dinner. She never showed up, and she's not answering her phone."

"Shit." He grabbed his own phone from his pocket and realized he must have turned it off at some point in the afternoon. He powered on the telephone and saw Lexie had called him not once but three times. "I'm out of here."

He called her as he made his way out of the restaurant, but she didn't answer. He dialed again as he waited for the valet to bring his car. She didn't pick up, and it was a long drive home, or felt like one, as he hit every traffic light on his route.

He finally reached his apartment and let himself inside. "Lexie!" he called out, walking quickly toward the bedrooms, finding her in his room, where they slept.

"I am so sick and tired of Keith's bullshit coming back to haunt me!" She threw a pillow across the room in frustration.

He bent down and picked it up, joining her on the bed. "What's wrong?" he asked, concerned. He propped the pillow back against the headboard. "Lexie was looking for you earlier. She thought you'd come to dinner."

"I tried. I was on my way, actually, when our friend Vincent Bernardi showed up."

"What?"

"Apparently those numbers on the drive were for accounts, and when he went to get his money, it was gone. Thank you, Keith."

"Fuck." He pinched the bridge of his nose, a head-ache already forming.

"Exactly. And guess who he thinks should pay him back?" She met his gaze. "I'm just so tired of Keith coming back to haunt me. And he has no right to expect you to pay off your brother's debts. It's just wrong."

Lucas shook his head. "I was wrong for thinking he'd just go away." Anger filled him. "I'd pay him if I thought that would be the end of it. I'd do anything to protect you and you know it. I'm just afraid he'd be back for more and we'll be in no better shape than we're in now." He let out a groan. "I think it's time we did some digging into those accounts."

"What? How?"

"I made a copy of what was on the drive." He shrugged. "Call it habit, but I always back things up for safekeeping. I'll send it over to Double Down Security and see what they come up with. I'll also give them everything I can on my brother. Maybe Keith had other accounts. One way or another, we need information to take to the police. This money isn't legal, and that's the only way to get Bernardi off our backs for good."

She twisted her hands and nodded.

He pulled her into a hug, inhaling her fragrant scent. "I agree. And I'm reinstating security."

She winced at that. "I hate knowing someone's watching my every move. But it's better than Bernardi coming near me again."

"I know. And I'm sorry I called them off."

"No, we both thought it was over. But I'm beginning to think it never will be."

LUCAS WAS THIS close to paying Bernardi and being done with it. The only thing that held him back was the obvious fact that if he paid the man once, he might come back for more. And more. He'd never be out of

Maxie's life, and that was unacceptable. Her safety was his ultimate priority.

So while Tyler Dare's men searched, Lucas focused on things at home. And he knew something was bothering Maxie. Something beyond the obvious fact that they still had to deal with the looming threat of Vincent Bernardi, a hovering ghost over their emotional and mental states.

But he could sense her distraction was about *more* than Keith's past haunting her. She was out of sorts, not in her usual good mood, and when he questioned her, she said she was just busy on the job and more tired than usual.

Too tired for sex.

He didn't pressure her, instead immersing himself in work and waiting on information. They were working on decoding the information on the drive, and once they accomplished that, they were looking into each account they found.

Lucas was sitting at his desk three days later when he got the call from Tyler Dare.

"Thank God. What do you have for me?" Lucas asked, hoping for good news.

"If I didn't have the best guy in the business, he never would have found it. Your brother stashed money in the Caymans."

Lucas jumped up from his seat, practically doing a

fist pump at the news. "Thank you."

"I'm sending you the information priority over-night. Not risking anything in email."

"You more than earned your money. Thank you again." Lucas couldn't wait to tell Maxie. After which, next stop was the cops.

LUCAS AND MAXIE called the police, detailing Bernardi's actions from the first time he'd accosted Maxie at the Halloween party and Lucas had met him at the gym to the present. The man already had a record, and the police were all too ready to believe their story. Especially since the authorities were monitoring his actions. They still hadn't given up on getting him on embezzlement and racketeering charges.

They'd been in a diner, meeting with a plainclothes detective so as not to call attention to the police in case Bernardi was watching. Hours had passed, of phone calls and conversation, when finally Aaron Gold, a Fed in a suit, presented them with a plan.

"You'll give Bernardi the account number and bank information in the Caymans. We'll work with our counterparts overseas and be there to take him into custody when he tries to access the account. Easy."

"Too easy," Lucas muttered, but he couldn't deny the relief flowing through his veins.

Maxie placed her hand in his, her own release of tension palpable. "And you'll contact us when he's in custody?" she asked.

Gold nodded. "You'll have done your part, and it'll be over," he assured her.

"Fine," Lucas said. "Anything to get this son of a bitch out of our lives."

Gold walked out and Lucas turned to Maxie. "Could it be that easy?"

"He sure made it sound that way." Maxie wound a strand of her long hair around her finger. "God, I don't even care if *you* hand Bernardi the information at this point. I want this over with, and I don't want to see him again. Ever."

He braced a hand on her knee, leaned in close, and brushed his lips over hers. "As soon as they have people set up in the Caymans, they'll call and tell us to pass over the information. It'll be a fast swap like the last time and he'll be gone. Keith's mess will finally be behind us. Then we can move forward with our lives."

He slid his hand up her thigh and she stiffened.

He stifled a curse and removed his hand. He didn't know what was going on with her or how to break through the wall she'd put up. For no reason, as far as he could tell. But his gut told him not to push. Not until this outside stress was behind them and they could truly focus on what was important.

Them.

Twenty-four hours later, Lucas got the phone call to deliver the account information to Bernardi. Grateful Maxie didn't want any part of the exchange, he met the man outside Blink.

"You're handing me cash out in the open like this?" Bernardi asked.

"No. I'm handing you my brother's secret account in the Caymans." Lucas held out a piece of paper with the information written on it. "This account has your money. The amount you told Maxie she owed you. Go find a way to retrieve it, and get the fuck out of our lives."

Bernardi stared at the paper in Lucas' hand, as if he was undecided. Clearly he'd thought he'd be getting cash out of Lucas.

Well, tough shit. "That's the money you asked for. It's the best you're going to get from me. I'm sure you'll have no problem managing to finagle your way in to claim that money. Regardless, I'm out. Done."

Bernardi snatched the sheet from his hand. "It's been a pleasure doing business with you and your lady."

Lucas frowned, watching as the large man walked away. With any luck, never to be seen again.

WHILE WAITING FOR word that Bernardi had been taken into custody in the Caymans, Lucas kept security on Maxie and his parents. He was no longer worried, certain the man had left the country, but having bodyguards was the prudent thing to do.

Waiting kept him busy. Not busy enough, because he still drove himself crazy over the way Maxie had withdrawn. It reminded him of the time after she'd lost the baby, only not quite as dark.

He struggled to find a way to approach her, but he didn't want to drag her back to that time for no reason. Everyone was entitled to downtime. Maybe work was hard on her.

Or maybe she was feeling confined, living with him, sleeping with him, and she needed space. He considered that possibility and discarded it, if only because Maxie was strong enough to tell him if the relationship wasn't working for her. She certainly hadn't held back when he'd fucked up.

None of which helped him figure out what was bothering her now.

Or what to do about it.

Finally, bright and early in the morning, Gold called him with the news that Bernardi had been taken into custody by island police at the Cayman Island's bank while trying to access Keith's bank accounts. Lucas assumed they would extradite him to the U.S.

He didn't know the details and he didn't care. Gold promised that with the information they'd amassed, the man was going away for a good long time.

That same day, Maxie begged him to let the body-guards go, and with Gold's assurances, there didn't seem to be a reason to keep them on.

MAXIE SCHEDULED A doctor's appointment with her old obstetrician, needing to confirm her pregnancy before she accepted it in her mind and could bring herself to discuss it with Lucas. She was exhausted, not sleeping, worried about being pregnant, concerned she couldn't carry to term and the doctors wouldn't know it until it was too late.

She feared accepting the idea of this baby, getting emotionally attached, something she thus far refused to let herself do, and having her heart and guts ripped out again. And thanks to her worries, depression was beginning to settle over her like an unwelcome, long-lost friend.

Fate was on Maxie's side. The day of her ob-gyn appointment, she found out Bernardi was out of her life for good, and she could finally put Keith behind her. And she could go to this appointment without worry that a bodyguard would report back to Lucas about where she was. She wanted to tell him on her terms, in her own time.

She headed to the doctor's office, a medical building with multiple doctors on every floor, and exited on three. She checked in, and after a little while waiting, she was brought into the exam room, where she undressed and put on a robe. She sat twisting her hands, trying to remain calm, when the doctor finally walked in.

"Maxie, I'm so happy to see you again." Dr. Mendez had been her regular obstetrician with her first pregnancy.

She hadn't been on call the night she'd lost the baby. Dr. Mendez was a pretty, dark-haired woman in her late thirties, and Maxie had always been drawn to her warmth and caring.

"How have you been?" the doctor asked.

"Umm … things have been a little crazy lately," Maxie said, thinking that was an understatement.

Dr. Mendez laughed. "Well, let's see what's going on. Now remember what I told you when you came to my office after … last time. There was nothing you could have done to prevent the miscarriage, and you aren't in a high-risk category should you get pregnant again. Of course, we can discuss extra testing…"

The doctor went on, but Maxie's ears were ringing, and she had trouble focusing. Just one reason she shouldn't have come alone.

"So let's move on to the exam. Your urine test already confirmed that you're pregnant, but let's do an exam and put your mind at ease."

Maxie's palms were sweaty as, a few awkward minutes later, she found herself in an all-too-familiar position, on the doctor's examining table with a sonogram screen to her side.

Alone.

Keith had never made the time to go with her to her appointments, and she'd chosen not to have Lucas here today. Something she'd regretted the minute she stepped into the room and the walls seemed to close in on her.

The doctor chatted as she worked, and soon Maxie saw the flickering on the screen and the tiny image of her baby staring back at her. Her stomach flipped, and at that moment, she realized she'd been lying to herself. She didn't have to worry about getting attached to this baby. She already was.

The child was a product of love, and she'd been wrong to let her fears overcome her emotions. She blinked back tears.

"Are you okay?" Dr. Mendez asked, handing Maxie a tissue.

She wiped at her eyes. "Yes. Does everything look okay?" she asked, almost afraid to hear the answer.

"Perfect. Because it's so early, you'll have to come

back in a few weeks to hear the heartbeat. Eight weeks. You're about at four." The doctor grasped her hand. "I know how stressful this pregnancy is going to feel. Please come back any time. Call me if you need anything. Next time, make a list of questions and bring someone to help you remember the answers."

Maxie sniffed, the tears running down her face unchecked. All she wanted now was to get home and tell Lucas he was going to be a father.

She dressed and took the elevator back downstairs, in even more of a daze than she'd been in before. She would have preferred to head straight over to Lucas' office, but she had to work, so she'd have to settle for telling him at home tonight.

No, she realized. Work had to wait. Now that she'd wrapped her head around the notion, she had to share the news and tell Lucas they were having a baby. He deserved to be there from the beginning, and this was as close to that as she could give him.

Her fears weren't gone, and she'd need every bit of his support to get through the next eight months. Not that she couldn't handle whatever life threw at her alone, but she chose not to. And that was the difference between her relationship with Keith and the one she shared with Lucas.

She'd been coming around, beginning to understand it before the pregnancy news had blindsided her and put her in a state of frozen fear. But while lying on the exam table, looking at that tiny blip on the screen, clarity had descended over her.

She wanted this baby, and she wanted to raise him or her with the man she loved. All of which meant she had a lot of explaining to do after withdrawing and pushing him away. He deserved so much better than what she'd been giving him, and from now on, she intended to give him everything. Her whole heart.

She stepped onto the curb, but before she could turn toward the subway entrance, someone grabbed her arm and pulled her roughly against him.

"You and your boyfriend have been more trouble than you're worth," a familiar voice said in her ear. "Act normal. We're taking a walk."

Fear raced through her, but she did as he said, managing to put one foot in front of the other. "I don't get it. They said you were in custody!"

He yanked her closer to him and continued down the street. "When something looks too easy, it usually is, and I didn't get where I am without being damned careful. No way was I going to do the pickup and risk getting arrested," he muttered. "Moron island cops picked up a dummy looking to make a buck who looked like me."

Gold hadn't waited for actual confirmation they had the right man before letting Maxie and Lucas think they were off the hook. She bit the inside of her cheek, Bernardi's rough grip dragging her along.

"What do you want with me now?" she asked.

He stopped but held on to her tightly, meeting her gaze. "You're my ticket out of this country. Your boyfriend is going to give me the money I need to disappear before the Feds fingerprint the guy they have in custody and come looking for me."

She blinked back tears. "You're going to what? Kidnap me?" She pressed her hand over her belly. "Please, I'm pregnant. Just let me go. I'll make sure Lucas pays you this time. I—"

"No more games or trust," he snarled. "Let's go. My car's on the next corner."

Maxie knew she couldn't go anywhere with him. Her only chance was to escape him now, when there were people around to see and hear her scream. Or pass out.

She slowed her feet. "I'm not feeling well," she said, forcing him to shorten his steps.

Panic threatened to overwhelm her, but she thought about the baby inside her and the life she could have if she survived. *Don't get into a car with a kidnapper.* She knew this.

"Come on." He yanked on her arm.

At that moment, she let her knees buckle and slid to the ground.

"Fuck!" He yanked so hard on her arm he nearly pulled it out of the socket, but she kept her body weight close to the ground, unwilling to be his victim. "Help!" she screamed, knowing the street wasn't packed but had people walking by.

"You stupid bitch!" He leaned down, getting so close his fetid breath hit her nostrils. "Get up."

"No." She spat in his face and lay down close to the sidewalk, unwilling to give him any leverage to haul her up and drag her with him.

He slapped her hard, her head hitting the concrete.

He pulled out a gun and aimed it at her stomach. "You really think I'm going to jail?"

Before she could answer, which wouldn't be easy given the way her head was spinning, someone tackled Bernardi, slamming him to the ground by her side.

His gun fell from his hand and skidded across the sidewalk. She grabbed it, holding it on him with shaking hands. A crowd had formed around them, and a tall man knelt down beside her. "Here. Let me," he said in a kind voice as he extended his hand.

She gave him the weapon, collapsing to the ground in relief.

Chapter Eleven

Lucas, Kade, and Derek sat with Blink's accountants, listening to them drone on about expenses, taxes, and other things, which Lucas tuned out, his mind elsewhere. With all that had been going on in his life, it was a miracle he still had a business, but he had his partners to thank for stepping up when he had other problems going on.

Tonight he planned to corner Maxie and find out what was bothering her, once and for all. They had nothing if they didn't have honesty. She would have to spill her guts, and he was going to have to be man enough to hear it.

His cell rang mid-meeting. He'd forgotten to turn off the ringer, another testament to his focus being elsewhere.

"Sorry." He pulled it out of his pocket, planning to shut it off when Gold's name came up on the screen—the Fed who'd given him the all clear this morning.

"Excuse me," he said to the others in the room, answering before he'd walked out. "Monroe."

"Mr. Monroe, it's Federal Agent Gold."

Lucas' skin began to tingle uncomfortably. "What's wrong?"

The other man cleared his throat. "There was a mix-up in the Caymans. The island police picked up a man who looked like Vincent Bernardi as he was trying to access your brother's account. But when my men arrived to take custody, it wasn't the right man."

"Fuck!" Lucas exploded. "Are you kidding me?"

The agent groaned into the phone. "My men knew it wasn't Bernardi immediately, but we don't have jurisdiction there. We had to let the locals make the arrest."

Lucas thought his head might detonate, so great was his anger. "Well, you didn't have to tell me it was a done deal and he was in custody until you knew for sure."

Lucas' hands began to shake as he realized he had to call Maxie. "You'd better hope Bernardi hasn't gotten to Maxie, or I'm going to make sure you lose your job and reputation."

He cut off the call and dialed Maxie's cell phone, but it went directly to voice mail as it sometimes did when she was at work. He wasn't reassured and called Nick Power, Maxie's boss, on his cell.

"Nick, it's Lucas Monroe," Lucas said when Nick answered on the first ring.

"What can I do for you?" Nick asked.

Lucas ran a trembling hand through his hair. "I know I sound like a crazy man, but can you ask Maxie to call me? It's urgent," Lucas said, his heart pounding in his chest for reasons he couldn't put into words.

Logic said he had time to get in touch with her, but his gut screamed something else.

"Andrea, can you give Maxie a message?" Lucas heard Nick ask someone in the office.

He couldn't hear the rest of the conversation.

"Okay, as soon as she's back from her doctor's appointment, Andrea will let her know," Nick said.

"Thanks," Lucas said numbly and disconnected the call. Doctor? She hadn't mentioned an appointment at any time this week or when he'd dropped her off at work this morning.

Not that he needed to know everything, but when he added her behavior to her secrecy, his feeling of unease grew. Was she sick and hiding it from him? he wondered, his stomach churning.

Okay, he thought, trying to calm himself down. He needed to prioritize. First up, he needed to let her know about Bernardi, so he called her back and left a message to call him, that it was urgent. Then he dialed Tyler Dare and had him work on getting security in place again as soon as possible.

Unable to bring himself to rejoin the business meeting in the conference room, he headed for his office, where he paced the floors. Nothing about today made sense, and he wasn't comfortable.

At all.

Kade and Derek met up with him after their meeting ended, shutting themselves in his office, giving them privacy.

"Hey, man. What's wrong?" Derek asked.

"The Feds fucked up and I can't locate Maxie." He explained the phone call and Maxie's unexpected, at least to Lucas, doctor's appointment. "My skin is itching like something is seriously wrong."

Kade frowned. "Want me to ask Lexie if she knows anything?"

"Would you? I'm losing my mind."

Kade pulled out his phone and made the call. "Hey, baby. Have you heard from Maxie?" He listened, glanced at Lucas, and shook his head.

Shit.

Lucas forced himself to breathe.

Kade wrapped up the call and refocused on the problem at hand. "Try her cell again," he said, not once questioning Lucas' gut or worry, which he appreciated.

He walked over to his desk, where he'd placed his cell, and the phone rang. He answered immediately.

"Mr. Monroe? This is Officer Jones. I'm calling at the request of Ms. Maxie Sullivan."

His heart almost stopped beating, and he lowered himself into his chair. "What happened?"

His friends immediately surrounded him.

"We're still sorting out details, but she's being taken by ambulance to Lenox Hill Hospital. You can meet her there."

Kade insisted on taking his driver. The man always insisted on the finer things in life, and a little while later, Lucas sat in an emergency room, waiting for news on Maxie. And because he wasn't related or her husband, he couldn't demand to be let in to see her until the doctors were good and ready.

It was déjà vu all over again.

If he hadn't already seen the result of Kade's fist hitting a hard wall, he'd be tempted to do some punching of his own. As it was, he was stuck feeling helpless while time passed slowly and he could do nothing but wait. At least this time he wasn't alone. Kade and Derek had accompanied him here, along with Lexie, who'd met them. Understanding he didn't want to talk, they provided moral support and left him to brood in peace.

An officer had stopped by to question Lucas about Vincent Bernardi and had filled Lucas in on what had happened to Maxie outside the doctor's office. Lucas was furious that the man had gotten near Maxie again, and if he hadn't wanted to be here the minute he could see her, he would've been at Gold's office wringing the man's neck. As it was, Lucas directed the police to Gold for more information. If it was the last thing Lucas did, he'd make sure the man lost his job.

He couldn't begin to imagine Maxie's fear and panic when Bernardi had grabbed her, but he admired that she was smart enough not to go with the man and to take the risk to fight him in public. He clenched and unclenched his fists, the hands on the clock on the wall dragging as they moved.

The longer he sat, the further back his thoughts traveled, to the night she'd called him when she'd lost the baby. The panicked trip to the hospital. The long, interminable time alone in a small room with ancient magazines as he waited for news. And he came to one solid conclusion.

This was the last time he'd be kept away from Maxie because they weren't married. They were damn well going to work through her issues and get married as soon as possible. In his book, their *I love yous* weren't new, they were years in the feeling … and they'd wasted enough time apart.

"Mr. Monroe?" A nurse walked through the door and called out his name.

Lucas nodded. "That's me."

His friends turned, as eager for news as he was.

"You can come back and see Ms. Sullivan now."

Lucas expelled a long breath of relief. "I'll fill you guys in as soon as I can," he promised, and followed the woman through the double doors.

They passed a row of closed curtains and finally came to the corner cubicle. "In here. She's expecting you," the nurse said.

Lucas nodded. "Thank you." His heart galloped inside his chest as he pushed the curtain aside and stepped into the small enclosed area.

Maxie lay on a hospital bed, her head back against the pillows, her skin pale. A slight bruise marred one cheek, and anger swamped Lucas along with a sense of futility that he hadn't been there to prevent her from getting hurt. Logically he knew he couldn't be with her every minute of every day, but in this case, his anger was warranted. He'd relied on false information, and she'd been out alone, exposed to Bernardi.

He quietly stepped into the room, and she stirred, her big brown eyes settling on his. In that one instant, he affirmed that she was everything he wanted and cared about, and he'd do anything to fix whatever had been wrong over the last several weeks or so.

Anything to make her his for good.

★   ★   ★

MAXIE WAS DIZZY and her head hurt, but there was no better sight than Lucas walking in. She'd been asking for him for the past hour, but they'd insisted on checking her for injuries and making sure the baby was okay. She'd have been happier if Lucas had been here the entire time. But at least he was here now.

He strode over and clasped her hand, but it wasn't enough. The next thing she knew, his arms were wrapped solidly around her, holding her tight, and the tears she'd been holding back since Bernardi had approached her fell freely.

"I'm sorry," she said, sniffling against his shirt.

"For what?" He pulled back and met her gaze, all the worry he'd been through in his expression, all the love he felt for her in his eyes.

She swallowed hard. "For how I've acted lately."

A corner of his mouth kicked up in a half smile. "We'll get to that."

He brushed her hair off her face, studying her intently. "Are you really okay?"

She nodded, regretting it immediately. The pain seared through her skull. "Just a bad headache."

"Are you up to telling me what happened?"

She wasn't ready to tell him about the baby. Not

until this mess with Keith was out and behind them. "Bernardi walked up to me on the street, grabbed my arm, and said I was coming with him. That the cops in the Caymans got a decoy he sent instead of going himself because he suspected a trap. I started walking with him, but the minute I saw the car, all the TV talk shows I've seen telling you not to get into a vehicle and go to a second location with a kidnapper came back to me. I knew I'd risk anything to stay where I was."

"Smart girl," he murmured.

She shrugged, trying not to remember the abject fear and just relay the story. "I let myself go limp and fell to the ground, lying down flat. He was so angry. He tried to yank me up, and when I wouldn't go, he slapped me. That's when my head hit the concrete."

A low growl escaped Lucas' throat. "Are you okay?"

"They're watching me for a concussion."

He pulled in a deep breath. "What happened next?"

"Next thing I knew, someone tackled him, throwing him off me. His gun fell near me, I grabbed it…"

His entire body trembled. "Jesus. And I thought there was nothing worse than getting the phone call from Gold telling me they'd gotten the wrong guy. I tried to reach you. I kept dialing. Eventually I called

Nick, who said you were at a doctor's appointment," Lucas said, his gaze narrowing, as if that piece of information had been lost in his panic and he was just now remembering it.

Her face flushed with heat. "Right. About that…"

He pushed himself onto the edge of the bed, scooting in beside her. "You don't have to report your every move to me, but—"

She drew a deep breath. "It's all tied to how I've been acting lately."

She drew nervous circles on the hospital blanket. "It turns out I'm pregnant." She paused to let that piece of information sink in.

He blinked. "Pregnant."

"Yep."

"As in having a baby. My baby."

She caught herself before nodding. "Yes. And I didn't handle the news well at all. After everything I went through last time, I panicked. I couldn't imagine living every day of the next nine months wondering when something was going to go wrong. I was petrified of losing the baby, of the pain, the depression, the hurt, the loss." Tears were flowing freely now.

He brushed them away with his thumb, looking dazed himself. "Are you telling me you were at the doctor to… end the pregnancy?" he asked, the words sounding torn from his throat.

"No! No. I never once considered that possibility."

The tension eased from his face, and his entire body fell lax in relief.

"It's odd, actually. I never considered anything. It's like I went numb to everything around me. I could only focus on what I couldn't handle, and I felt like I was slipping back into the black hole that consumed me in those early days."

"So where were you today?"

She realized he hadn't yet expressed his feelings about the baby, but this wasn't a normal set of circumstances, and she needed to give him time. Time to understand her and the hurt she'd inflicted these last weeks.

"I was at the doctor confirming the pregnancy."

"You went alone?" Hurt flickered in his gaze and her heart cracked open.

How could she have done this to him? He'd been nothing but giving, kind, and loving. Willing to open himself and his heart to her, and she'd kept him in the dark.

There was nothing she could say to make it better.

She could only tell him her truth and hope he would forgive. "The minute I sat down in the room, undressed in that gown, and waited for the doctor, I knew I'd made a huge mistake. I wanted you there as much as I realized I wanted the baby."

He remained silent, so she continued.

"I left the office planning to come straight to you and fill you in, but then…"

"Bernardi," they said at the same time.

She let out a nervous laugh.

Lucas didn't say another word, and in the silence, she began to wonder if she'd pushed him too far, hurt him too much. Everyone had their limits, and in not telling him about the baby, maybe she'd surpassed his.

She curled her hands into fists, digging her nails into her skin. She'd thought losing another baby was the worst thing that could befall her, but she realized now there was something equally devastating.

Losing Lucas.

MAXIE MIGHT HAVE a concussion, but Lucas was the one whose head was spinning now. A baby? She'd been pulling away because they were having a baby? Of all the scenarios that had gone through his mind, Maxie being pregnant hadn't been one of them.

"Lucas, say something. Please. I'm sorry I pushed you away, and I never would have terminated the pregnancy," she reiterated. "I swear it never crossed my mind."

He grasped her hand and looked into her eyes. "Maxie, you have to understand we have nothing if we don't have honesty. You don't have to be happy about something, but you can't keep something so important to us to yourself. You can't push me out in some misguided attempt at independence."

"I know why you'd think that, but this had nothing to do with standing on my own. You'd already proven to me how much you value me and that you allow me to make my own choices. This was sheer panic. I fell back into that depression that—"

"Shh." He placed a hand over her lips. "I know and I understand. I'm not angry. I'm overwhelmed. And before I even begin to express how else I'm feeling, I want things crystal clear between us."

She blinked, her eyes big and wide. "Okay."

"I need to know you trust me enough to come to me when something's wrong. No matter how big or scary."

She nodded. "Yes. I understand that now. I swear. I've made mistakes but I love you."

"I love you too, beautiful." He grinned now, big and wide. "A baby?"

"You're happy?" she asked.

"Not completely." As long as he had her where he wanted her, he was going for the full monty.

Her bottom lip trembled, and he didn't want to torture her. "Do you know why I wasn't here with you earlier?" he asked.

She shook her head, her eyes narrowed in confusion.

"Because we aren't married. I'm not your husband. I'm not legally the person who can make decisions for you or be told about your condition. So no, I'm not completely happy."

Sudden understanding lit her gaze along with a spark of happiness and excitement he hadn't seen in too long. "Say what you mean, Mr. Monroe."

He tipped his head back and laughed, knowing that finally, everything was as it should be. As it should have been since they were silly teenagers unwilling to admit their feelings.

"If I'm going to be a father, you're going to have to make an honest man out of me," he said with a wink.

"Oh, Lucas."

He gently clasped the back of her neck and eased her forward until their lips touched. He slid his mouth over hers ever so lightly and whispered, "Will you marry me?"

A salty tear slipped between them, and he leaned back, capturing it with his tongue.

"Yes," she said, wrapping her arms around him in a grip so tight he might never extricate himself. Which was a good thing, because he didn't want to.

"Thank God," he muttered. They'd finally gotten it

right. Finally found their time.

"Excuse me." The same nurse who'd led him in here poked her head in.

Lucas pulled back. "Yes?" he asked, trying not to sound annoyed.

"I have people here who are demanding to see Ms. Sullivan. I really can't have more than one or two at a time in here," she said.

He turned to Maxie. "Kade, Derek, and Lexie are here," he said.

"That's so sweet. Go get them," she said, poking Lucas in the shoulder. "We have our whole lives to be alone. And not in a hospital cubicle."

He growled his objection but he understood. His friends had been waiting for word, putting up with his worry and mood.

"Fine."

Besides, she was right. They had their whole lives.

A WEEK AFTER the incident with Bernardi, Maxie dressed for a dinner out with Lucas. She hadn't had a concussion, but to appease him and the doctors, she'd taken the rest of the week off from work to rest. After a few days in the house, she was dying to get out of the apartment. Lucas promised a special night, and he'd made a reservation at an exclusive restaurant that usually booked out months in advance.

She chose a fitted black dress she probably wouldn't be able to wear much longer and a pair of heels. She finished her makeup and had just completed curling the bottom of her hair when Lucas came up behind her in the bathroom.

He clasped his hands around her waist and pressed a soft kiss to her neck before sliding his palms across her stomach. "You know I'm going to be here for everything. Every doctor's appointment, every kick."

"Every midnight craving?" she asked with a laugh. She was trying to focus on being positive and not thinking about the past or scary possibilities.

"Every last one," he promised.

From the second he'd found out she was having their baby, Lucas had done a pretty darn good job helping her, always making her laugh, showing her how excited he was, how much he loved her. She'd done the same, determined to never hurt him or push him away again.

She stepped back and took him in. He looked incredibly sexy in a pair of black pants and a white dress shirt, unbuttoned enough to reveal his tanned skin and light sprinkling of chest hair she enjoyed running her fingers over at night.

"Stop looking at me like that or we'll miss our reservation," he said on a low rumble.

"You can pick up right here when we get home." Her stomach chose that moment to let out a very unattractive hungry rumble. "I'm not only eating for two, I'm hungry for two," she said, feeling her cheeks flame.

"Let's go. I need to feed you both."

She swiped a hint of gloss on her lips and let him lead the way.

To her surprise, he'd hired a car service for the night. "I want everything about tonight to be special," he said, his breath warm and sexy in her ear.

It was so wonderful not to have to focus on anything but being happy, the past and Keith permanently in their rearview mirror. Happiness was something she was getting used to, but Lucas made it easy.

The car pulled up to the restaurant, and Lucas helped her out, leading her inside with a hand at her lower back.

He gave their name to the maître d'. "Right this way, Mr. Monroe. I have a private table for you in the back, just like you requested."

Feeling special and very loved, she walked to the back, leaning against Lucas as they made their way to the table.

"Surprise!" a loud group of people yelled out, and Maxie blinked, jerking back into Lucas.

Kade and Lexie, Kendall, Derek, her friend Bailey

and her boyfriend, and to Maxie's utter surprise, Lucas' parents were there as well.

"What's going on?" she asked, glancing up at Lucas.

"We waited a long time for our time. To get things right. And I thought you'd want to be around people who love you when we celebrate."

She wrinkled her nose. "Celebrate what?"

"Our official engagement," he said, reaching into this pocket and pulling out a small black box.

She sucked in a shallow breath. She'd agreed to marry him at the hospital, but she hadn't been sure it wasn't a spur-of-the-moment question born of frustration that he hadn't been able to get in to see her. They hadn't discussed it again since.

Clearly he'd been planning though.

He popped open the box, revealing a huge round stone in a classic Tiffany setting. "Lucas!"

"I might not always act like I'm a billionaire, but my wife is going to look like she's married to one." He lifted the ring from the box.

She couldn't help but notice his hand was shaking, which endeared her to him even more. Because she was trembling too. How could she not be when all her dreams were finally coming true?

He knelt down on one knee. "Maxie Sullivan, I have loved you my entire life and plan to love you for eternity. Will you marry me?"

Her eyes welled up, threatening to ruin the makeup she'd put on so carefully. "Yes. Of course!" She held out her hand.

He slipped the ring onto her finger, where it fit perfectly. "Lucas, I love it and I love you."

He rose and leaned in for a kiss, which resulted in a round of applause from their company, who she'd almost forgotten was there.

A glance told her everyone looked happy for them, including his mother and father.

"How'd you manage your parents being here?" she asked quietly.

"Believe it or not, that was easy. In the end, they don't want to lose their family. They love you." He pulled her against him, heedless of the people waiting to congratulate them. "And so do I."

With that pronouncement, he kissed her again, for a long, long, long time.

Preorder the next Billionaire Bad Boy's story (Derek's story) in GOING DOWN HARD.

Billionaire Bad Boys:
Rich, Powerful and sexy as hell.

Derek West rose from poverty to take the tech world by storm. He's sexy, confident and has no problem making a play for the opposite sex. He never anticipates that the one woman who has him going down hard, is going to make this bad boy work for what he wants … and needs.

Thank you for reading **GOING DOWN FAST**. I would appreciate it if you would help others enjoy this book too. Please recommend to others and leave a review.

Meet the Dares!
Dare to Love –
Book 1 Dare to Love Series –
(Ian Dare)

Keep up with Carly and her upcoming books:

Website:
www.carlyphillips.com

Sign up for Carly's Newsletter:
www.carlyphillips.com/newsletter-sign-up

Carly on Facebook:
www.facebook.com/CarlyPhillipsFanPage

Carly on Twitter:
www.twitter.com/carlyphillips

Hang out at Carly's Corner! (Hot guys & giveaways!)
smarturl.it/CarlysCornerFB

CARLY'S MONTHLY CONTEST!

Visit: www.carlyphillips.com/newsletter-sign-up and enter for a chance to win the prize of the month! You'll also automatically be added to her newsletter list so you can keep up on the newest releases!

Dare to Love Series Reading Order:

Book 1: Dare to Love (Ian & Riley)

Book 2: Dare to Desire (Alex & Madison)

Book 3: Dare to Touch (Olivia & Dylan)

Book 4: Dare to Hold (Scott & Meg)

Book 5: Dare to Rock (Avery & Grey)

Book 6: Dare to Take (Tyler & Ella)

*each book can stand alone for your reading enjoyment

DARE NY Series (NY Dare Cousins) Reading Order:

Book 1: Dare to Surrender (Gabe & Isabelle)

Book 2: Dare to Submit (Decklan & Amanda)

Book 3: Dare to Seduce (Max & Lucy)

*The NY books are more erotic/hotter books

Read on for an excerpt of **Dare to Love**,
Ian and Riley's story.

Dare to Love

Excerpt

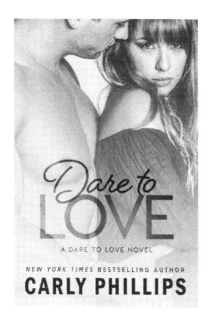

Chapter One

ONCE A YEAR, the Dare siblings gathered at the Club Meridian Ballroom in South Florida to celebrate the birthday of the father many of them despised. Ian Dare raised his glass filled with Glenlivet and took a sip, letting the slow burn of fine scotch work its way down his throat and into his system. He'd need another before he fully relaxed.

"Hi, big brother." His sister Olivia strode up to him and nudged him with her elbow.

"Watch the drink," he said, wrapping his free arm around her shoulders for an affectionate hug. "Hi, Olivia."

She returned the gesture with a quick kiss on his cheek. "It's nice of you to be here."

He shrugged. "I'm here for Avery and for you. Although why you two forgave him—"

"Uh-uh. Not here." She wagged a finger in front of

his face. "If I have to put on a dress, we're going to act civilized."

Ian stepped back and took in his twenty-four-year-old sister for the first time. Wearing a gold gown, her dark hair up in a chic twist, it was hard to believe she was the same bane of his existence who'd chased after him and his friends until they relented and let her play ball with them.

"You look gorgeous," he said to her.

She grinned. "You have to say that."

"I don't. And I mean it. I'll have to beat men off with sticks when they see you." The thought darkened his mood.

"You do and I'll have your housekeeper short-sheet your bed! Again, there should be perks to getting dressed like this, and getting laid should be one of them."

"I'll pretend I didn't hear that," he muttered and took another sip of his drink.

"You not only promised to come tonight, you swore you'd behave."

Ian scowled. "Good behavior ought to be optional considering the way he flaunts his assets," he said with a nod toward where Robert Dare held court.

Around him sat his second wife of nine years, Savannah Dare, and their daughter, Sienna, along with their nearest and dearest country club friends. Missing were their other two sons, but they'd show up soon.

Olivia placed a hand on his shoulder. "He loves her, you know. And Mom's made her peace."

"Mom had no choice once she found out about *her.*"

Robert Dare had met the much younger Savannah Sheppard and, to hear him tell it, fallen instantly in love. She was now the mother of his three other children, the oldest of whom was twenty-five. Ian had just turned thirty. Anyone could do the math and come up with two families at the same time. The man was beyond fertile, that was for damned sure.

At the reminder, Ian finished his drink and placed the tumbler on a passing server's tray. "I showed my face. I'm out of here." He started for the exit.

"Ian, hold on," his sister said, frustration in her tone.

"What? Do you want me to wait until they sing 'Happy Birthday'? No thanks. I'm leaving."

Before they could continue the discussion, their half brother Alex strode through the double entrance with a spectacular-looking woman holding tightly to his arm, and Ian's plans changed.

Because of *her.*

Some people had presence; others merely wished they possessed that magic something. In her bold, red dress and fuck-me heels, she owned the room. And he wanted to own her. Petite and curvy, with long, chocolate-brown hair that fell down her back in wild curls, she was the antithesis of every too-thin female he'd dated and kept at arm's length. But she was with his half brother, which meant he had to steer clear.

"I thought you were leaving," Olivia said from beside him.

"I am." He should. If he could tear his gaze away from *her*.

"If you wait for Tyler and Scott, you might just relax enough to have fun," she said of their brothers. "Come on, please?" Olivia used the pleading tone he never could resist.

"Yeah, please, Ian? Come on," his sister Avery said, joining them, looking equally mature in a silver gown that showed way too much cleavage. At twenty-two, she was similar in coloring and looks to Olivia, and he wasn't any more ready to think of her as a grown-up—never mind letting other men ogle her—than he was with her sister.

Ian set his jaw, amazed these two hadn't been the death of him yet.

"So what am I begging him to do?" Avery asked Olivia.

Olivia grinned. "I want him to stay and hang out for a while. Having fun is probably out of the question, but I'm trying to persuade him to let loose."

"Brat," he muttered, unable to hold back a smile at Olivia's persistence.

He stole another glance at his lady in red. He could no more leave than he could approach her, he thought, frustrated because he was a man of action, and right now, he could do nothing but watch her.

"Well?" Olivia asked.

He forced his gaze to his sister and smiled. "Because you two asked so nicely, I'll stay." But his attention remained on the woman now dancing and laughing with his half brother.

RILEY TAYLOR FELT his eyes on her from the moment she entered the elegantly decorated ballroom on the arm of another man. As it was, her heels made it difficult enough to maneuver gracefully. Knowing a devastatingly sexy man watched her every move only made not falling on her ass even more of a challenge.

Alex Dare, her best friend, was oblivious. Being the star quarterback of the Tampa Breakers meant he was used to stares and attention. Riley wasn't. And since this was his father's birthday bash, he knew everyone here. She didn't.

She definitely didn't know *him*. She'd managed to avoid this annual party in the past with a legitimate work excuse one year, the flu another, but this year,

Alex knew she was down in the dumps due to job problems, and he'd insisted she come along and have a good time.

While Alex danced with his mother then sisters, she headed for the bar and asked the bartender for a glass of ice water. She took a sip and turned to go find a seat, someplace where she could get off her feet and slip free of her offending heels.

She'd barely taken half a step when she bumped into a hard, suit-clad body. The accompanying jolt sent her water spilling from the top of her glass and into her cleavage. The chill startled her as much as the liquid that dripped down her chest.

"Oh!" She teetered on her stilettos, and big, warm hands grasped her shoulders, steadying her.

She gathered herself and looked up into the face of the man she'd been covertly watching. "You," she said on a breathy whisper.

His eyes, a steely gray with a hint of blue in the depths, sparkled in amusement and something more. "Glad you noticed me too."

She blinked, mortified, no words rushing into her brain to save her. She was too busy taking him in. Dark brown hair stylishly cut, cheekbones perfectly carved, and a strong jaw completed the package. And the most intense heat emanated from his touch as he held on to her arms. His big hands made her feel small, not an easy feat when she was always conscious of her too-full curves.

She breathed in deeply and was treated to a masculine, woodsy scent that turned her insides to pure mush. Full-scale awareness rocked her to her core. This man hit all her right buttons.

"Are you all right?" he asked.

"I'm fine." Or she would be if he'd release her so she could think. Instead of telling him so, she continued to stare into his handsome face.

"You certainly are," he murmured.

A heated flush rushed to her cheeks at the compliment, and a delicious warmth invaded her system.

"I'm sorry about the spill," he said.

At least she hoped he was oblivious to her ridiculous attraction to him.

"You're wet." He released her and reached for a napkin from the bar.

Yes, she was. In wholly inappropriate ways considering they'd barely met. Desire pulsed through her veins. Oh my God, what was it about this man that caused reactions in her body another man would have to work overtime to achieve?

He pressed the thin paper napkin against her chest and neck. He didn't linger, didn't stroke her anywhere he shouldn't, but she could swear she felt the heat of his fingertips against her skin. Between his heady scent and his deliberate touch, her nerves felt raw and exposed. Her breasts swelled, her nipples peaked, and she shivered, her body tightening in places she'd long thought dormant. If he noticed, he was too much of a gentleman to say.

No man had ever awakened her senses this way before. Sometimes she wondered if that was a deliberate choice on her part. Obviously not, she thought and forced herself to step back, away from his potent aura.

He crinkled the napkin and placed the paper onto the bar.

"Thank you," she said.

"My pleasure." The word, laced with sexual innuendo, rolled off his tongue, and his eyes darkened to a deep indigo, an indication that this crazy attraction she experienced wasn't one-sided.

"Maybe now we can move on to introductions. I'm Ian Dare," he said.

She swallowed hard, disappointment rushing through her as she realized, for all her awareness of him, he was the one man at this party she ought to stay away from. "Alex's brother."

"Half brother," he bit out.

"Yes." She understood his pointed correction. Alex wouldn't want any more of a connection to Ian than Ian did to Alex.

"You have your father's eyes," she couldn't help

but note.

His expression changed, going from warm to cold in an instant. "I hope that's the only thing you think that bastard and I have in common."

Riley raised her eyebrows at the bitter tone. Okay, she understood he had his reasons, but she was a stranger.

Ian shrugged, his broad shoulders rolling beneath his tailored, dark suit. "What can I say? Only a bastard would live two separate lives with two separate families at the same time."

"You do lay it out there," she murmured.

His eyes glittered like silver ice. "It's not like everyone here doesn't know it."

Though she ought to change the subject, he'd been open, so she decided to ask what was on her mind. "If you're still so angry with him, why come for his birthday?"

"Because my sisters asked me to," he said, his tone turning warm and indulgent.

A hint of an easier expression changed his face from hard and unyielding to devastatingly sexy once more.

"Avery and Olivia are much more forgiving than me," he explained.

She smiled at his obvious affection for his siblings. As an only child, she envied them a caring, older brother. At least she'd had Alex, she thought and glanced around looking for the man who'd brought her here. She found him on the dance floor, still with his mother, and relaxed.

"Back to introductions," Ian said. "You know my name; now it's your turn."

"Riley Taylor."

"Alex's girlfriend," he said with disappointment. "I saw you two walk in."

That's what he thought? "No, we're friends. More like brother and sister than anything else."

His eyes lit up, and she caught a glimpse of yet another expression—pleasantly surprised. "That's the best news I've heard all night," he said in a deep, compelling tone, his hot gaze never leaving hers.

At a loss for words, Riley remained silent.

"So, Ms. Riley Taylor, where were you off to in such a hurry?" he asked.

"I wanted to rest my feet," she admitted.

He glanced down at her legs, taking in her red pumps. "Ahh. Well, I have just the place."

Before she could argue—and if she'd realized he'd planned to drag her off alone, she might have—Ian grasped her arm and guided her to the exit at the far side of the room.

"Ian—"

"Shh. You'll thank me later. I promise." He

pushed open the door, and they stepped out onto a deck that wasn't in use this evening.

Sticky, night air surrounded them, but being a Floridian, she was used to it, and obviously so was he. His arm still cupping her elbow, he led her to a small love seat and gestured for her to sit.

She sensed he was a man who often got his way, and though she'd never found that trait attractive before, on him, it worked. She settled into the soft cushions. He did the same, leaving no space between them, and she liked the feel of his hard body aligned with hers. Her heart beat hard in her chest, excitement and arousal pounding away inside her.

Around them, it was dark, the only light coming from sconces on the nearby building.

"Put your feet up." He pointed to the table in front of them.

"Bossy," she murmured.

Ian grinned. He was and was damned proud of it. "You're the one who said your feet hurt," he reminded her.

"True." She shot him a sheepish look that was nothing short of adorable.

The reverberation in her throat went straight to Ian's cock, and he shifted in his seat, pure sexual desire now pumping through his veins.

He'd been pissed off and bored at his father's ridiculous birthday gala. Even his sisters had barely been able to coax a smile from him. Then *she'd* walked into the room.

Because she was with his half brother, Ian hadn't planned on approaching her, but the minute he'd caught sight of her alone at the bar, he'd gone after her, compelled by a force beyond his understanding. Finding out she and Alex were just friends had made his night because she'd provide a perfect distraction to the pain that followed him whenever his father's other family was near.

"Shoes?" he reminded her.

She dipped her head and slipped off her heels, moaning in obvious relief.

"That sound makes me think of other things," he said, capturing her gaze.

"Such as?" She unconsciously swayed closer, and he suppressed a grin.

"Sex. With you."

"Oh." Her lips parted with the word, and Ian couldn't tear his gaze away from her lush, red-painted mouth.

A mouth he could envision many uses for, none of them tame.

"Is this how you charm all your women?" she asked. "Because I'm not sure it's working." A teasing smile lifted her lips, contradicting her words.

He had her, all right, as much as she had him.

He kept his gaze on her face, but he wasn't a complete gentleman and couldn't resist brushing his hand over her tight nipples showing through the fabric of her dress.

Her eyes widened in surprise at the same time a soft moan escaped, sealing her fate. He slid one arm across the love seat until his fingers hit her mass of curls, and he wrapped his hand in the thick strands. Then, tugging her close, he sealed his mouth over hers. She opened for him immediately. The first taste was a mere preview, not nearly enough, and he deepened the kiss, taking more.

Sweet, hot, and her tongue tangled with his. He gripped her hair harder, wanting still more. She was like all his favorite vices in one delectable package. Best of all, she kissed him back, every inch a willing, giving partner.

He was a man who dominated and took, but from the minute he tasted her, he gave as well. If his brain were clear, he'd have pulled back immediately, but she reached out and gripped his shoulders, curling her fingers through the fabric of his shirt, her nails digging into his skin. Each thrust of his tongue in her mouth mimicked what he really wanted, and his cock hardened even more.

"You've got to be kidding me," his half brother

said, interrupting at the worst possible moment.

He would have taken his time, but Riley jumped, pushing at his chest and backing away from him at the same time.

"Alex!"

"Yeah. The guy who brought you here, remember?"

Ian cursed his brother's interruption as much as he welcomed the reminder that this woman represented everything Ian resented. His half brother's friend. Alex, with whom he had a rivalry that would have done real siblings proud.

The oldest sibling in the *other* family was everything Ian wasn't. Brash, loud, tattoos on his forearms, and he threw a mean football as quarterback of the Tampa Breakers. Ian, meanwhile, was more of a thinker, president of the Breakers' rivals, the Miami Thunder, owned by his father's estranged brother, Ian's uncle.

Riley jumped up, smoothing her dress and rubbing at her swollen lips, doing nothing to ease the tension emanating from her best friend.

Ian took his time standing.

"I see you met my brother," Alex said, his tone tight.

Riley swallowed hard. "We were just—"

"Getting better acquainted," Ian said in a seductive tone meant to taunt Alex and imply just how much better he now knew Riley.

A muscle ticked in the other man's jaw. "Ready to go back inside?" Alex asked her.

Neither one of them would make a scene at this mockery of a family event.

"Yes." She didn't meet Ian's gaze as she walked around him and came up alongside Alex.

"Good because my dad's been asking for you. He said it's been too long since he's seen you," Alex said, taunting Ian back with the mention of the one person sure to piss him off.

Despite knowing better, Ian took the bait. "Go on. We were finished anyway," he said, dismissing Riley as surely as she'd done to him.

Never mind that she was obviously torn between her friend and whatever had just happened between them; she'd chosen Alex. A choice Ian had been through before and come out on the same wrong end.

In what appeared to be a deliberately possessive move, Alex wrapped an arm around her waist and led her back inside. Ian watched, ignoring the twisting pain in his gut at the sight. Which was ridiculous. He didn't have any emotional investment in Riley Taylor. He didn't do emotion, period. He viewed relationships through the lens of his father's adultery, finding it easier to remain on the outside looking in.

Distance was his friend. Sex worked for him. It

was love and commitment he distrusted. So no matter how different that brief moment with Riley had been, that was all it was.

A moment.

One that would never happen again.

RILEY FOLLOWED ALEX onto the dance floor in silence. They hadn't spoken a word to each other since she'd let him lead her away from Ian. She understood his shocked reaction and wanted to soothe his frazzled nerves but didn't know how. Not when her own nerves were so raw from one simple kiss.

Except nothing about Ian was simple, and that kiss left her reeling. From the minute his lips touched hers, everything else around her had ceased to matter. The tug of arousal hit her in the pit of her stomach, in her scalp as his fingers tugged her hair, in the weight of her breasts, between her thighs and, most telling, in her mind. He was a strong man, the kind who knew what he wanted and who liked to get his way. The type of man she usually avoided and for good reason.

But she'd never experienced chemistry so strong before. His pull was so compelling she'd willingly followed him outside regardless of the fact that she knew without a doubt her closest friend in the world would be hurt if she got close to Ian.

"Are you going to talk to me?" Alex asked, breaking into her thoughts.

"I'm not sure what to say."

On the one hand, he didn't have a say in her personal life. She didn't owe him an apology. On the other, he was her everything. The child she'd grown up next door to and the best friend who'd saved her sanity and given her a safe haven from her abusive father.

She was wrong. She knew exactly what to say. "I'm sorry."

He touched his forehead to hers. "I don't know what came over me. I found you two kissing, and I saw red."

"It was just chemistry." She let out a shaky laugh, knowing that term was too benign for what had passed between her and Ian.

"I don't want you to get hurt. The man doesn't do relationships, Ri. He uses women and moves on."

"Umm, Pot/Kettle?" she asked him. Alex moved from woman to woman just as he'd accused his half brother of doing.

He'd even kissed *her* once. Horn dog that he was, he said he'd had to try, but they both agreed there was no spark and their friendship meant way too much to throw away for a quick tumble between the sheets.

Alex frowned. "Maybe so, but that doesn't change

the facts about him. I don't want you to get hurt."

"I won't," she assured him, even as her heart picked up speed when she caught sight of Ian watching them from across the room.

Drink in hand, brooding expression on his face, his stare never wavered.

She curled her hands into the suit fabric covering Alex's shoulders and assured herself she was telling the truth.

"What if he was using you to get to me?"

"Because the man can't be interested in me for me?" she asked, her pride wounded despite the fact that Alex was just trying to protect her.

Alex slowed his steps and leaned back to look into her eyes. "That's not what I meant, and you know it. Any man would be lucky to have you, and I'd never get between you and the right guy." A muscle pulsed in Alex's right temple, a sure sign of tension and stress. "But Ian's not that guy."

She swallowed hard, hating that he just might be right. Riley wasn't into one-night stands. Which was why her body's combustible reaction to Ian Dare confused and confounded her. How far would she have let him go if Alex hadn't interrupted? Much further than she'd like to imagine, and her body responded with a full-out shiver at the thought.

"Now can we forget about him?"

Not likely, she thought, when his gaze burned hotter than his kiss. Somehow she managed to swallow over the lump in her throat and give Alex the answer he sought. "Sure."

Pleased, Alex pulled her back into his arms to continue their slow dance. Around them, other guests, mostly his father's age, moved slowly in time to the music.

"Did I mention how much I appreciate you coming here with me?" Obviously trying to ease the tension between them, he shot her the same charming grin that had women thinking they were special.

Riley knew better. She *was* special to him, and if he ever turned his brand of protectiveness on the right kind of woman and not the groupies he preferred, he might find himself settled and happy one day. Sadly, he didn't seem to be on that path.

She decided to let their disagreement over Ian go. "I believe you've mentioned how wonderful I am a couple of times. But you still owe me one," Riley said. Parties like this weren't her thing.

"It took your mind off your job stress, right?" he asked.

She nodded. "Yes, and let's not even talk about that right now." Monday was soon enough to deal with her new boss.

"You got it. Ready for a break?" he asked.

She nodded. Unable to help herself, she glanced over where she'd seen Ian earlier, but he was gone. The disappointment twisting the pit of her stomach was disproportional to the amount of time she'd known him, and she blamed that kiss.

Her lips still tingled, and if she closed her eyes and ran her tongue over them, she could taste his heady, masculine flavor. Somehow she had to shake him from her thoughts. Alex's reaction to seeing them together meant Riley couldn't allow herself the luxury of indulging in anything more with Ian.

Not even in her thoughts or dreams.

About the Author

Carly Phillips is the *N.Y. Times* and *USA Today* Bestselling Author of over 50 sexy contemporary romance novels featuring hot men, strong women and the emotionally compelling stories her readers have come to expect and love. Carly's career spans over a decade and a half with various New York publishing houses, and she is now an Indie author who runs her own business and loves every exciting minute of her publishing journey. Carly is happily married to her college sweetheart, the mother of two nearly adult daughters and three crazy dogs (two wheaten terriers and one mutant Havanese) who star on her Facebook Fan Page and website. Carly loves social media and is always around to interact with her readers. You can find out more about Carly at www.carlyphillips.com.

CARLY'S BOOKLIST

by Series

Billionaire Bad Boys Reading Order:

Book 1: Going Down Easy

Book 2: Going Down Fast

Book 3: Going Down Hard

Dirty, Sexy Reading Order:

Book 1: Dirty Sexy Saint

Book 2: Dirty Sexy Inked

Book 3: Dirty Sexy Cuffed

Book 4: Dirty Sexy Sinner

Dare to Love Series Reading Order:

Book 1: Dare to Love (Ian & Riley)

Book 2: Dare to Desire (Alex & Madison)

Book 3: Dare to Touch (Olivia & Dylan)

Book 4: Dare to Hold (Scott & Meg)

Book 5: Dare to Rock (Avery & Grey)

Book 6: Dare to Take (Tyler & Ella)

*each book can stand alone for your reading enjoyment

DARE NY Series (NY Dare Cousins) Reading Order:

Book 1: Dare to Surrender (Gabe & Isabelle)

Book 2: Dare to Submit (Decklan & Amanda)

Book 3: Dare to Seduce (Max & Lucy)

*The NY books are more erotic/hotter books

Unexpected Love Series

The Right Choice

Suddenly Love

Perfect Partners

Unexpected Chances

Worthy of Love

Carly's Earlier Traditionally Published Books

Serendipity Series

Serendipity

Destiny

Karma

Serendipity's Finest Series

Perfect Fit

Perfect Fling

Perfect Together

Serendipity Novellas

Fated

Hot Summer Nights (Perfect Stranger)

Bachelor Blog Series

Kiss Me If You Can

Love Me If You Dare

Lucky Series

Lucky Charm

Lucky Streak

Lucky Break

Ty and Hunter Series

Cross My Heart

Sealed with a Kiss

Hot Zone Series

Hot Stuff

Hot Number

Hot Item

Hot Property

Costas Sisters Series

Summer Lovin'

Under the Boardwalk

Chandler Brothers Series

The Bachelor

The Playboy

The Heartbreaker

Stand Alone Titles

Brazen

Seduce Me

Secret Fantasy

Made in the USA
Lexington, KY
16 October 2016